paper airplane

unique tales from a mile high

Kersten L. Kelly

Talisman Book Publishing LLC, Chicago

talismanbookpublishing.com

Published by Talisman Book Publishing LLC, Chicago

paper airplane: unique tales from a mile high. Copyright © 2013 by Kersten L. Kelly. All rights reserved.

talismanbookpublishing.com

Designed by Kersten L. Kelly

Library of Congress Catalog Number: 2012954426

ISBN-13: 978-0-9853487-2-4
ISBN-10: 0-9853487-2-0

Printed in the United States of America

For Joe and Cooks. My two best friends, mentors, and the people I look to when things just don't make sense. Thanks for the clarity, support, love, and immeasurable fun together.

A Note From The Author

I began the journey of a lifetime the very first time I stepped foot on an airplane. The simple task of being transported from one destination to another became so much more. I started meeting random passengers that taught me some of the most impactful lessons of my life. I kept a detailed notebook of the sights, sounds, stories, and characters that crossed my path. Little did I know, the collection of stories would inevitably end up as this novel. Many of my fellow passengers were unforgettable for their own reasons. Despite my purpose for travel or final destination, I emerged with the same message many times: *you never know what you will learn on an airplane.*

My journey is relived through this memoir. The messages in these anecdotes will evoke a variety of emotions. The rollercoaster ride of the highest highs and some of the lowest lows appeals to readers of all genres. I'm most certainly not the first passenger with a tale to tell from an airplane, and I probably won't be the last. There will always be a more intense, unusual, or dramatic story. This book is merely my collection of unique tales from a mile high.

Contents

Preface   15

Chapter One   19
The Beginning of A+ Airlines

Chapter Two   27
Vance, the Gap Commercial Superstar

Chapter Three   39
Ira, the Hungry Watchdog

Chapter Four   55
Mandy, the Inspirational Model

Chapter Five   67
Harry, the Most Humble Football Fan

Chapter Six   79
Howard, the Nomadic Businessman

Chapter Seven   89
Jonah, the Philanthropic Sailor

Chapter Eight   107
Kenny, the Floating Jeweler

Chapter Nine   123
Doctor Curlson, the Romantic Chemist

Chapter Ten   135
Mark, the Morning Drunk

Chapter Eleven   147
Estelle, the Tattooed Actress

Chapter Twelve   157
Saint Anthony, the Lucky Finder

Chapter Thirteen   167
Roger, the Crabby Splasher

Chapter Fourteen   175
John, the Paternal Soldier

Chapter Fifteen   189
Cathy, the Chatty Civilian

Chapter Sixteen   197
Jack, the Heart Throb

Chapter Seventeen   207
The Final Descent

Epilogue   215
Acknowledgments   219
About the Author   223

Preface

Writing and publishing a book has always been on my bucket list. I was able to check that item off the list when I published my first book, *economics: a simple twist on normalcy*, in March of 2012. That book is a compilation of pop culture, social media, history, education, and business, dissected through the lens of economic theory. It delves into explanations of why and how markets change and how certain goods influence the way others are demanded and supplied. With *economics*, I was targeting a fairly specific market, and the timeliness of the publication was critical to its success.

The book was published at a time when the brunt of the economic recession was over, yet people were more confused than ever in regard to the financial future of the world. The United States was in a state of slow recovery from the economic recession of 2008. People were cautious about the market, about buying and selling property, and about the notion of starting from ground zero in a new career. Hundreds of nuances occurred during the lapse in the economy that deserved to be recorded in history.

My ploy was to take this a step further and help explain some of these nuances through an economic perspective. It was a relatable book for readers interested in the nonfiction genre, with a particular focus on business and the economy. This didn't mean every reader would be interested in reading the book. For those who were looking for less education and more entertainment in their book choice (i.e. anyone who doesn't dig a read on the economy), I recognized an opportunity to publish again.

During the long journey of publishing my first book, I learned all of the necessary steps that went into the process. I was an organic publisher, so everything was a development. Early on, I recognized that in order to get the word out, I needed readers to provide feedback on their opinions of the book. As I was querying for reviewers and marketing help*, I found that every person I asked preferred different types of stories.

Some liked fiction books, some sought out young adult series, and yet others preferred genres that I hadn't ever delved into reading, let alone writing. I received a handful of promises to review the book, and out of that bunch, only a fraction was able to fulfill their commitment. The entire progression from start to finish was a mixture of highs and lows with one very specific lesson at the end: my economics book does not appeal to everyone.

Some readers wanted to lose themselves in the traits of the characters. Others wanted to picture the scenes in their imagination, and the rest yearned to relish in the possibility of experiencing the plot firsthand. Even though the readers were after different things, there was one overarching commonality among many of the individuals I contacted: They wanted a story. My first book did not fit this bill.

---

* Reviews are the single most valuable (and free) form of advertising for a book. The validity of a review coming from another human being cannot be reproduced. Popular opinion is important, and people like to know what others think about any product or service. It is intrinsic in the human race to seek others' opinion when choosing, even if it's just selecting what book to read.

A nonfiction economics book is technical and objective by its very nature. I couldn't promise that readers would have a warm, fuzzy feeling when they reached the end of the book, but that was not my intention for it. I still craved the chance to give people a story instead of explaining theories. I wanted the challenge of a different style of writing, one that readers could directly relate to emotionally. I wanted a second chance at a new style of writing.

The process of publishing was long and challenging, but I couldn't get enough of it! I had so much fun writing, marketing, and promoting my first book that I just had to start the process all over again. I am more than just a nonfiction writer though, and I saw the opportunity to share some of my experiences in the format of a semi-fiction book.

The stories in this book are actual firsthand accounts of what I experienced. Some of these accounts have been passed on to me, stories I felt compelled to include. Each played on my slew of emotions, as I am sure they will touch yours. It is human nature to want a feel-good ending to a story.

I can't promise that for all of these, but there are a few gems sprinkled in the mix. One thing I can promise is that you will take away important messages that have proven to resurface in my life over and over.

paper airplane is mostly factual. However, since I am designating it a semi-*fiction* book, names, characters, places, and events have the potential to be fictitious. I tried my best to remember accurate depictions of the stories, but I am only human. I also attempted to preserve any privacy and/or defining characteristics of the people included in these tales. My goal is not to reveal any personal information that would allow a reader to depict who the person is. I want to make this clear up front so readers do not have misconceptions about my goals.

I did take the time to choose the characters' names, values, and attributes with great distinction to uphold the special meaning they held for me. I will request only a few things as you read this book: Sit back, relax, and enjoy. Some of the stories you are about to read are highly entertaining. I only hope you can enjoy reading them as much as I have enjoyed living, compiling, and composing them…

Chapter One

The Beginning of A+ Airlines

When I was a kid in grammar school, I was the quintessential teacher's pet. I thought of school as a competition and strived to be the best student in my class and stand out in any way I could amongst my fellow peers. Every time my teachers asked a question, I raised my hand higher than others. I would simultaneously yelp and wave my hand around in an effort to attract the teacher's attention, so enthused was I with the idea that I might be chosen to answer a problem or read a paragraph aloud, taking that honor from my classmates. In each and every one of my classes, every single year, I wanted to be the best student ever.

I turned my completed homework in a few days before it was due and begged to help my teachers with odd jobs around the classroom. I stayed in during recess to cut out and hang the various seasonal decorations that adorned the room. I volunteered to clean chalkboard erasers, pick up messy construction-paper catastrophes, and organize the plethora of crayons and markers – a relative dirty job since many of them were missing their caps. I inevitably ended up with rainbow-colored fingers, but I didn't care; it was an honor and a source of pride to be asked to help my teacher in any capacity. That was where I found my niche as a young person, and I was good at it.

I had a great sense of humor about being the overachiever of the classroom and embraced that role wholeheartedly. During the holiday season, I made sure my mom bought a better gift for my teacher than she bought for my dad. Why? Because showering my teacher with delicious chocolates and homemade goodies, all bundled up with festive holiday-themed wrapping paper and garland and bows, would earn me a good reputation. If I wanted to be the best student, I had to bring my A-game all the time, and I milked that for all it was worth.

Whenever my teacher made the slightest adjustment to her appearance – a haircut or a new dress, for instance – I made sure to shower her with compliments. When she brought in photos of her family, her dog, or her house, I told her how lovely they all were. I exaggerated about how well she'd coordinated the 1980s-themed haircut with her tapered, white-washed jeans. Any sort of compliment, true or false, was part of my gig. I was the epitome of the definition of a teacher's pet, and I was proud of it.

My brown-nosing reputation was well known among my peers. I lived in a quaint little town just outside of Chicago. The population of only 28,000 people meant it was relatively simple to get to know most of the kids I went to school with at an early age. Many of the same 150 kids I started kindergarten with were standing next to me at my high school graduation. My mom knew their moms, and they all mingled and clucked with one another during Market Day pickup, a quintessential scene from classic suburbia.

There was nothing extraordinary about the structural format of my elementary school. There were four classrooms per grade, and each year, the rosters for the classrooms were shuffled around and redistributed to the new set of teachers. It was always a nerve-racking first day of school to find out which kids were in my classroom. Whether or not my best friend would make it into my classroom was an absolute crapshoot. If not, I knew I was in for a long school year, for I'd have to wait for recess every day to gossip with her. To a child in grade school, those few hours between morning bell and recess seemed like a never-ending eternity, an elementary form of torture, and gossip was something that couldn't wait!

The second-most-important unknown on the first day was whether or not any of the bullies were to be seated in my class with me all year. They always snickered one-liners to push my buttons and purposely annoyed me and the other "smart"* kids. I just assumed they were jealous and tried my best to ignore their name-calling and immature, attention-seeking antics. As a brown-noser, I prepared myself for the ridicule from my fellow classmates who were not so selflessly gifted. I earned my A's by being an obsequious servant to my instructors.

Fifth grade was one year of grammar school that I got stuck in the same class with (in my opinion) the worst bully. He somehow weaseled his way into my class every year and knew just how to get under my skin. He refused to leave me alone, no matter how many times I told on him. He thrived on the ability to pick on me relentlessly, and he was good at it. Even though I was able to brush off the majority of his nonsensical banter, there was one collision that I physically could not ignore. He got me that time.

Although the incident occurred many moons ago, I still get a major kick out of the practical joke and find myself reiterating the anecdote whenever a friend is in need of a good laugh.

One day, I was being particularly attentive to the lesson my teacher was presenting. I was being especially responsive to every question she asked. As I remember it, I dominated the class participation, to the point where the other kids in class didn't even bother to raise their hands. It almost became irrelevant for anyone else to partake because I was able to singlehandedly

---

*   "Smart" is being used synonymously with suck-up. I just thought it sounded more sophisticated.

answer everything for everyone. Most of the kids lost their enthusiasm for the lesson, and a dull lull surfaced among the daydreaming youngsters – the perfect scenario for a bully in need of attention.

The lethargic aura of that classroom didn't last long. All of a sudden, the bully threw an object across the room, smacking me right in the forehead. No, a stray crayon did not somehow spontaneously generate wings and fly across the room to nail me in the noggin. Instead, my favorite bully had thrown an expertly crafted paper airplane at me. Initially, I was appalled by his rude gesture. I rolled my eyes at him and scoffed at the very thought of what he had done.

After I regained my bearings and composed myself, I picked up the airplane in disgust and simultaneously shot him a dirty look. After all, I had to stand up for myself. I was ticked off that some jerk thought he had the right to try to shut me up by throwing an inanimate object at my head – but then I took a closer look at the airplane. The plane had a large emblem on the side of it, branded as "A+ Airlines."

Without even thinking, I couldn't help but burst out into a boisterous laugh. *A+ Airlines?* As annoying as that bully was 99.9 percent of the time, he gained some credibility with me for that rather well-thought-out prank of his. It was just plain funny. There was no secret about my overachieving personality. I embraced it and had no problem boasting it whenever I could.

As a response to my incessant answers to my teacher's questions, the airplane had a very defined purpose that it was able to accomplish: to shut me up. I knew it was his way to make fun of me, but I didn't care. It was such a simple, ridiculous joke, yet it brilliantly sent a strong message. I couldn't help but appreciate the creativity that went into the slogan. I'll even argue that I took it as a compliment. *Is he implying that I'm so perfect that I deserve an A+?* Only I would have assumed that as a fifth-grader.

As I remember it, the entire class burst into an uproar, and the teacher got upset with us for being disruptive. She eventually convinced everyone to settle down, and we returned to our lesson. I'm sure I shot off some nasty looks to the bully in retaliation, but after that things went right back to normal, and I continued to answer questions.

I have never forgotten that story, and when I reminisce about it or retell it as an adult over cocktails or hors d'oeuvres, I try to add a charismatic edge to exaggerate it. I incorporate lots of exclamatory facial expressions and hand gestures to make it more entertaining for my audience. Most people have a very similar reaction to the one I did that day in fifth grade: genuine laughter. Maybe it's the addition of alcoholic beverages, but people seem to enjoy it.

No matter what town a person went to school in or region of the country they originated from, everyone (including me as an adult) understands the stereotypical annoyances of the teacher's pet. A practical joke that actually took some rational thought and ingenuity from a fifth grader impresses the majority of adults who hear about it, as well as myself. Mocking a teacher's pet with his own ammo (i.e. earning good grades and participating in class), coupled with a slight smack in the dome, is just funny and makes for a great ice-breaking anecdote.

Most of the adults who hear this story are able to relate to it. The tale ignites memories from people's own childhood experiences. Adults are able to step back to yesteryear for a moment, to be a kid again, if only for a split second. Depending on their own childhood demeanor, they may imagine themselves living vicariously through the bully and taunting "Sally, the brown-nose girl" who annoyed them while they were growing up.

Some might assimilate better with the eleven-year-old me who obsessively tried to outdo everyone. Whether they were the overly engaged student or the one folding a piece of paper to prepare it for takeoff, most people can reminisce about their childhood or, at the very least, enjoy the creativity of the practical joke. It's all relative to one's own experiences, as most stories in life are.

Clearly, that one day in the fifth grade impacted me in

some strange way if I am still pondering the incident and telling the story to others. The joke of it all is that, as an adult, I am a very frequent flier on real airplanes. Each time I enter the small capsule of metal that eventually launches into the air to end up in a completely new destination, I walk off those flights having learned something about the people I meet. I can't argue whether each ride will yield something positive, but something is indeed gleaned. My favorite bully sent a stronger message than he ever expected that day: You never know what you might learn on an airplane.

After years of meeting people and listening to their stories, I decided to share them with the world, similar to the passing around of the paper airplane anecdote. I wanted to write a lighthearted conglomeration of stories that tie together to create a depiction of people intertwined with sarcasm and humor. You should know that the majority of these stories had me walking away muttering, "Wow," under my breath – or at least thinking it. I cannot guarantee this reaction was always positive, but it was a wow reaction nonetheless. As you read on, I think you'll catch my drift.

This book is a compilation of the stories from many intriguing individuals whom I have met thus far, sitting in the closest quarters in public transportation: on an airplane. I've learned that my only option is to get comfortable being scrunched up next to a complete stranger in a seat with minimal leg room, cold beverages at my disposal, and limited space-saver restrooms. What other choice do I have for that two and a half hours, if not to engage in conversation with another human being who is in the same traveling-in-close-quarters predicament?

In my opinion, airplane rides can be mundane; it is imperative to find something interesting to keep your mind stimulated, so that we aren't all asking, "Are we there yet?" like impatient children on a summer family vacation. On many occasions, I've taken the time to converse with people instead of reading a book, attempting a crossword or word search, or listening to the same scrambled tunes on repeat on my iPod. I decided to comprise a book of the stories I've experienced while coasting through the clouds, a relatively lighthearted account of the diversity in the world. If all else fails, one can occupy their time on their next flight by reading this book.

For the last few years, I've kept a detailed journal of all of the stories I experienced and that my fellow passengers divulged while miles high in the sky. This is a holistic account of some of the most memorable people and narratives I've encountered and collected on various airplanes. I have also chosen to include a few tales from my close family and friends, definitely deserving to be included here. As you will soon find out, some of these stories are just too impactful to discard them into the abyss of forgotten history. Allow me to reiterate: You never really know what you might learn on an airplane!

For the respect and protection of the people I met, I have changed some of the names, places, and identifying descriptors that could possibly incriminate someone or link them to these stories. My goal is to keep the uniqueness of each of the stories whole, while preserving the privacy of those who have so willingly and generously shared their fascinating tales and experiences.

I also feel obligated to preface this entire book with an admission: I am a chronic exaggerator. Ever since I was a little kid, I've found that if I tell stories with a little bit of extra pizazz* to make them slightly more interesting, I receive a better reaction from my listeners. This trait has carried with me throughout my adult life. As a result, I cannot separate some of my embellishments from the stories you are about to read in this book. I implore you to take this with a grain of salt and enjoy these crazy stories I've experienced.

---

* By "pizazz," I'm referring to turning a number like 100 into 1,000. In my humble opinion – or perhaps in reality – people read and listen to stories to be entertained. Sometimes larger, bigger, and better just make for a more interesting anecdote. Many times, the people who know me best will call me out when I exaggerate something, in an attempt to keep me grounded – and I appreciate each and every one who does.

So, ladies and gentlemen, please fasten your safety belt around your lap by clasping the two metal clamps together and pulling tightly on the strap. Please put your tray tables in the upright, locked position, and prepare your stowaways underneath the seat in front of you for takeoff. We are expecting a quite a bit of turbulence, so do not move about the cabin until the captain turns off the "Fasten Seatbelt" sign. We have been cleared for departure. Sit back, relax, and enjoy the flight. We would like to thank you for choosing A+ Airlines. Welcome aboard!

Chapter Two

Vance, the Gap Commercial Superstar

One of my college friends and I celebrate an ongoing annual tradition that first debuted in March of 2006. It was a brisk end to the winter season, and most of my fellow peers were headed somewhere warm and sunny. I chose to venture into the great state of New York for the first time, and I've gone back at least once a year since.

I'll never forget that first year of the now-ongoing custom. Her family members are some of the most generous, down-to-Earth people I know. Being East Coast natives, they were happy to take us on a first-class scenic route through the city. The first stop was at a standard New York style delicatessen for an "everything" bagel smothered in fluffy, white cream cheese. The clerk offered to add lox and chives, but I took a pass on that quintessential food, already more than overwhelmed with the four pounds of bread oozing with cheese that was creating a damp area on the paper bag that contained it.

Once we were all carbed up and full of far more than our recommended daily allowance of dairy, we headed out to explore the city. Our trip was filled with the typical tourist activities that everyone's first time to the Big Apple should include.

We hopped on the Staten Island Ferry to float across the Hudson River for an up-close-and-personal view of a vast representation of pure American culture: The Statue of Liberty. I had never seen a figure as dominant, meaningful, or absolutely breathtaking in my entire life. The lady's burning gold torch glistens in the shining sun, and her long, flowing dress is symbolic of the patriotism and important history of the United States.

The history encompassed in her existence reminded me of when I was a kid in social studies class. All those hours my teacher spent drumming into our heads that it was a gift from the French finally found meaning when I was able to visualize, right there in front of me, the copper, cast iron, and steel lady I'd learned so much about.

After basking in the glory of her beauty and majesty, we moseyed over to a local favorite among thousands of residents. The next part of the tour de' New York City landed us on the edge of Central Park. My friend's parents wanted to make our experience special, and they had a surprise for us when we arrived: Her father hailed a carriage pulled by a flawless white horse. The driver helped us into our chariot and began to lead us on a picturesque trip around the park.

We basked through the trees and gazed at the others strolling through the park. It was such a picturesque start to the evening. We could even see hundreds of glistening stars above the carriage when we looked up. Truly, I felt like I was immersed in a fairytale. There really is nothing like a brisk, breezy ride through gorgeous natural scenery, giggling and clucking with some of my closest friends.

To complete our night, we hustled up to the fifty-seventh floor of one of the city's many skyscrapers. Lining the top of the cylindrical building is The View, a restaurant that rotates as patrons nibble on gourmet appetizers. It boasts gorgeous observations as it overlooks the entire illuminated city below. As if the delicious entrée of filet mignon and grilled asparagus over creamy mashed potatoes wasn't enough, the intricate desserts were dazzled and dripped with chocolate sauce and fresh raspberries as a garnish. Sitting under the stars, staring out at a city of bright lights and activity, was golden. Peering through those massive glass windows high above the world, I caught a glimpse of every part of that amazing city.

A shot I snapped of The Statue of Liberty

It was truly a storybook adventure, filled with boisterous laughs, mouth-watering food, idealistic scenery, and the best friends any person could ever ask for. Because it was such a phenomenal experience in every way, that trip became the commencement of an ongoing annual trip to New York to visit my friends. I can't help but love that city and the people I care deeply about who live there.

Each year, the plan has been slightly adjusted, different than the year before. the first trip had set the expectations quite high, so my friend always plans additional activities each visit to make the time memorable. We visited her favorite local Hibachi restaurant, she gave us a tour of the local malls, where we shopped until we literally dropped, and one year she planned a Memorial

Day party, complete with the grilling of juicy hamburgers, swimming in her crystal-clear pool, and lounging around on the patio with a cold brew in hand.

Another year, the trip took us to the sandy East Coast beaches for The New York Airshow. From our vantage point on Jones Beach, we gazed in awe at the aerodynamic jets that buzzed overhead and performed their gravity-defying flips. Every time I've ventured there, to the East Coast, there's been something unique that made my trip unforgettable. The best part is figuring out what it's going to be.

The yearly trip usually falls on our around Memorial Day, an automatic three-day weekend. In 2011, I was summoned a little later in the year to join my friend in celebrating her graduation from her master's program. The invitation she sent included a message about indulgence in some of my favorite gourmet cupcakes, so it was a no-brainer. She knows me well enough to know that I can always be bribed with delicious desserts.

My friend planned an extensive party for her friends and family at her parents' house on Long Island, complete with a disc jockey to play all the latest pop music. She hired a waitress to provide full-service delivery of scrumptious appetizers and a bartender to keep the patrons occupied with any mixed drink, beer, or spirits they might desire. How could anyone resist those amazing adornments, that atmosphere, and the celebration of such a distinguished accomplishment? I most certainly couldn't, so I made the plan to join her in the festivities. I booked my ticket on A+ Airlines, packed up my sundresses, flip-flops, a sparkly belt, and a few sweaters, just in case Mother Nature decided to throw a few chilly days in there. I was so excited to spend such a fun weekend with my friend.

After a few weeks of waiting, I raced to the airport after work and trekked through long lines at security. I stopped at the McDonald's, then sat down at my gate to eat my fast food and wait. I'd scored a ticket that would seat me in the emergency exit. Anyone who has ever been so blessed knows why this is a good thing. There was so much leg room that I could put my legs in a pike position, and they still didn't touch the seat in front of me. Don't get me wrong: I'm not a tall person, but anyone can appreciate a few extra inches of space in the confinement of a jumbo jet.

With all of my worldly belongings in hand, I made my way to the window seat of the emergency exit and plopped down on the chair beneath me. I buckled my seatbelt and opened the air vent over my head to stimulate circulation in the stagnant cabin. I settled into my place and noticed a young lady, about my age, sitting in the aisle seat of my row. She was dressed in business attire and had her laptop computer open in front of her. As she typed quickly, we exchanged a few smiles, and the passengers filed in like a herd of cattle.

Anyone accustomed to flying knows that the most uncomfortable, dreaded seat in any given row is the middle seat. The unfortunate passenger assigned to sit there is forced to be squished into minimal space between two complete strangers, both of whom may be taking up more than their fair share of the room. Although there are armrests to divide the seating into separate spaces, many commercial airline passengers do not adhere to the proper etiquette of giving their friendly neighbors any room. Since space is a very limited commodity, it is vital to be slightly selfish in dividing the territory among the rightful temporary owners.

I watched each and every passenger pass up the space that remained vacant between us. I initiated conversation with the young lady sitting next to me, and she eventually introduced herself as "Heather." We almost instantly connected on the subject of the horrible middle seat, rejoicing about the exorbitant amount of space the row provided us. Albeit boring, it was typical preflight banter for me. I was more than impressed with the gymnastic configurations I could still do with my legs in such a spacious row of seats. Truly, it's the little things in life!

While Heather and I exchanged introductory information, the final passengers began boarding the plane. A young man walked slowly toward the exit row and pointed to our row. He expressed his interest in the open seat and politely asked if anyone was sitting there. We shook our heads, smiled, and shuffled our belongings briefly as he shimmied into the tight area. I warned him that he was going to be sitting next to two chatty women, and he gave a half-hearted smirk of disgust and stared forward to the bulkhead of the plane.

In that instant, I knew we were going to be a burden to him. Because I am an extrovert at heart, I took it as a challenge to engage him in conversation and actually learn about his story. Initially, I judged his actions and lack of verbal communication to be an indicator of his bland personality. It was a stereotype to assume he'd be boring just because he wasn't an overly enthusiastic twenty-something looking forward to an exciting weekend of eating, drinking, and making merry with friends.

His appearance was ordinary. He sported hipster-style clothing, complete with a tight, button-down plaid shirt and tight-fitting skinny jeans. He coordinated that with some color variation of hi-top Converse All-Star shoes with the laces weaved up his leg. He looked annoyed at my incessant chitchat.

Nevertheless, the man I'd presumed to be boring ended up having one of the most interesting stories I've heard during the course of any mode of transportation. Little did I know that I was sitting next to a former celebrity, of sorts. After a few minutes of continuous conversation between me and Heather, we finally prompted an introduction from him by initiating a greeting, and he told us his name was "Vance."

I immediately began collecting meet-and-greet information from them. We all introduced ourselves to one another formally and shook hands. I asked them both what they did, and Heather answered first, stating she was a recruiter for an online nursing program for a major university on the East Coast. Her occupation required that she fly to accredited hospitals around the eastern half of the country and recruit potential students for the program. Thanks to sophisticated Internet software, distance-learning nurses were able to manage a fairly full class load while still gaining hands-on experience in the field.

Heather talked about the perks of her position; she'd quickly earned a status on A+ Airlines and had received many extra special benefits as a loyal and very frequent flier. She was able to test-drive every car on the market and had narrowed down her choices to the vehicle she actually owned by doing so. She picked flashy, red convertibles in cities with gorgeous weather and heavy-duty sport utility vehicles (SUVs) to plow through rugged terrain and brutal weather patterns.

She also built quite a repertoire of lodging in the best hotels. Whatever eastern city I named, she knew the premier place to stay – places that would do a lot more for her than leave the light on. I would have bet a couple thousands of dollars that she could have easily made a career switch to travel agent. When I told her that, she laughed.

By serving as the liaison between her school and the pool of nurses who were seeking their masters', Heather received an added benefit that could have, quite possibly, been considered invaluable: her own education for a master's in nursing came at no cost to her. She told me she'd wanted to work in the medical field since she was a little girl, but she couldn't imagine the burden of paying the high cost for that education out of pocket. Thus, she'd found the perfect solution. She could be involved in the profession that was her passion while working to earn her degree. The only investment she had to make was her time.

The gig required Heather to be on the road (or in the sky) for the majority of most weeks, but the outcome would be a vital key for her future. As she described her work and her situation, I nodded in sincere approval. It seemed like the ideal position for her to be in, and it was refreshing to hear about someone who'd really found their niche in life.

Next, it was Vance's turn. He began by telling about his full-time corporate job. He worked as a manager in some sort of information technology field for an East Coast-based company, and from what I could gather, he worked hard and was a dedicated employee. On the surface, the rather dull explanation of his daily life paralleled the person I'd first laid eyes on when he had sat down, and the unimpressed expression on my face most likely conveyed that. He continued talking, though, and told us that his past included more adventurous ways of generating income for himself, based on his raw talent. That piqued my interest, and I really keyed in on his story.

When Vance was in college, he responded to an advertisement for a talent competition. The query summoned participants with some sort of organic musical talent. As he described it, the producers of the show requested "unique ways to generate music for a jingle that would promote a popular clothing line." The clothing line happened to be The Gap, which boasts one of the most innovative marketing campaigns in the history of retail clothing stores. The jingles they developed when I was in middle school are still memorable to this day; clearly, the company made a lasting impression.

Vance told the two of us that he auditioned to perform his talent in the holiday commercial. He was accepted, his major claim to fame. Like any normal* person would, I asked him to elaborate on this talent of his.

It wasn't what he *said* next that surprised me, but what he *did*. At roughly 38,000 feet in the air, Vance cupped both of his hands in a circular motion near his lips. He opened his mouth and made an orbicular shape by stretching his cheek muscles vertically. He rapidly began clapping his hands together, pushing air pockets through his mouth while simultaneously moving his lips around. Without even realizing what had happened so quickly, I heard the familiar tune to "We Wish You a Merry Christmas" in a multi-toned whistle emanating from his mouth.

It took me a second to fully comprehend how he was emitting this sound from his windpipes. Once I realized what was going on, I initiated a round of applause. Heather quickly joined me, and we all ended the musical session in boisterous laughter. Other passengers began to look toward our row, but we

---

* By "normal," I am referring to anyone curious and intrusive enough to inquire about Vance's talent. Fortunately for Heather, I have no shame in asking personal questions of complete strangers.

couldn't be bothered. *How in the world is he able to generate flute-like chimes using nothing but variations in mouth movements?* I wondered. I don't consider myself to have very many natural talents, so Vance's made a sizeable impression on me.

Not only was I mesmerized by the trance-inducing sounds, but I decided I wanted to try it myself. I figured it would be simple to mimic his noises, and I was definitely an expert ˙˙on belting out the lyrics to "We Wish You a Merry Christmas" during the holiday season in my car. I wouldn't even have to sing for the tune to be recognizable.

I held my hands up the way Vance had and followed the master's lead. He was patient in showing both Heather and me how to properly cup our hands to glean the loudest sound from the clapping. Just as I was about to begin, he manipulated my hands a little higher up to the proper position. He instructed both of us to keep the shape of our mouths still while moving our tongues up and down to generate a variation of notes and pitches. I concentrated very hard, and began to clap my hands vigorously against one another.

My debut as a mouth-clapper was less than enthralling. Some sort of noise came out in a monotone pitch over and over again. Despite my valiant efforts, I was unable to change the notes that were escaping my mouth, so my rendition of that beloved old Christmas carol was unrecognizable. Heather and Vance laughed at my numerous attempts, all of which resulted in absolute failure. The harder I tried, the worse the noise sounded. I did not want to make an abrasive scene on the airplane, so I rerouted my energy back to Vance.

I began making requests, song after song, treating him like my own personal jukebox for private serenades of my favorite

---

** My melodious expertise is a result of many years of practice. I think I have a better-than-great chance at winning the first-place prize any singing competition for the "World's Worst Vocalist." As a child, my parents were always quite encouraging. They reminded me, "Don't quit your day job." anytime I dared sing them a tune, and I must say appreciated their honesty.

tunes. I went from genre to genre, from Michael Jackson's "Billie Jean" to Usher's "U Got It Bad," all the way to the classic "Happy Birthday." Vance nailed each and every melody with utmost conviction, and I was stunned.

Vance had a unique talent, and I was obviously not the only person who thought so. Once we finished goofing around, he told us more about The Gap commercial, a holiday-themed ad campaign based on exceptional individual talents. Vance was a perfect candidate for the segment because his mouth-clapping was a rare talent, and he tied it in to the holidays by selecting a well-known carol. He told us that when he auditioned, the judges had immediately loved the idea, and he received a callback for the shoot.

It was his fifteen minutes of fame, his brief moment to shine in a national advertisement for a well-known clothing line – a commercial that would be seen all over the world. I thought back to the commercials he was describing and how much I had enjoyed them. They were tailored to the general public's interest and were, therefore, highly impactful. I congratulated Vance on his accomplishments as a brand ambassador, especially at such a young age since he couldn't have been more than thirty-two. He laughed and told me how much he had enjoyed it.

My next series of questions for Vance revolved around the other famous campaigns he'd taken part in during his lifetime. While he'd competed in a few small, regional talent competitions, he'd never been offered a bigger gig than The Gap commercial.

I'd had my doubts about Vance as a person when he'd originally taken that seat between us, seeming stoic and somewhat rude. I'd shamefully misjudged his character simply because he was quiet and respectful. As it turned out, the man had a very unique story to tell, and the three of us trying to mouth-clap in unison made for some hilarious entertainment.

We sat there clapping our hands in front of our faces in rapid motions, attempting to make music or at least a few glorious notes. I'm sure our fellow passengers on the airplane just thought we were insane, but I hope they got as many laughs out of our antics as we did.

Heather, Vance, and I chatted for the rest of the short two-hour flight to New York, learning about each other's lives. Vance was vigorously searching for the love of his life. He spent time traveling to visit his friends and family. He had no ties to any geographical region and noted that he was willing to move if an opportunity called for it. Heather was married to her college sweetheart, whom she said was her best friend in the world. The couple had been married for a little less than two years and planned to begin a family in the near future.

Both individuals had a different story to tell, and we'd all walked very different paths, yet we all came together to share a few hours of laughter like we'd known each other for years. Oddly enough, on a voyage east to create memories with old friends, I ended up doing the same with new ones.

I cherished the time I spent with those two individuals. Whether I ever see them again or not, I now know what it requires to be involved with a jingle for The Gap; it is a rare talent that I most certainly do not possess. Lucky for all of those brand-loyal Gap consumers, my lack of musical inclination will prevent me from ever participating in those ads.

This is the way the world works. People have different capabilities for a reason. Vance had a gift, and he shared it momentarily with us. Just as he was a vital key to the success of the filming of the commercial, I am vital to that company as a consumer of the product.

Heather and Vance were a perfect start to my annual trip. At the beginning of this chapter, I wrote about all of the mesmerizing tourist traps that I fell in love with on my first journey to the Big Apple. It bears repeating: Every time I ventured to the East, there was something unique that made my trip unforgettable. Vance took the cake on this particular trip, for his story was truly one in a million. Fortunately for me, he was not the only intriguing individual I stumbled across throughout my journeys. There were many more along the way.

Chapter Three

Ira, the Hungry Watchdog

Throughout my travels in the world in 2011, I found myself on a long connection flight from Istanbul, Turkey to Chicago, Illinois. I was on the brink of completing my MBA, and the final requirement for my degree was a global adventure that landed me in another country.

I was enrolled in an extensive distance-learning program that provided students living and working all over the world with a way to virtually connect. It also provided full-time employees with the flexibility to simultaneously earn a higher degree while continuing to gain experience in the workforce. The program had a very rigid, standardized set of classes that every student was required to pass before a degree would be conferred upon them. Although there was not a huge variability in classes, toward the final stages in the program, students were allowed to choose their final two elective classes. I selected Global Management.

The class was a first-run pilot course that required a group of about twenty students to commit to the multi-country course format to run. It was structured to afford students the opportunity to study business tactics and practices in another country for the first six weeks of the course. During the first portion of the course, scholars wrote papers, read articles, viewed cultural videos, and interviewed natives of the country to learn and prepare for the in-country arrival.

I spent countless hours immersing myself in the material. During the entirety of the six-week pre-country forum, I gained a better understanding of the impact of global business in India, and I was theoretically ready to venture over to the country.

In order to fulfill the final part of the credit for the class, I flew to India to immerse myself in the culture and experience business firsthand for ten grueling days. There was an eight-and-a-half-hour time difference from Chicago, and my body never fully adjusted to the new sleeping schedule. I would wake up at two a.m., and my tired and utterly confused body perceived it to be six p.m. of the prior evening. Not only was I attempting to consume the cultural aspects of another country, but I was also learning business practices along the way. I was on overdrive.

At times, I felt delirious and confused due to extreme exhaustion, food deprivation, and adjustment to a completely different climate (and world, for that matter). By the end of the trip, I was more than ready to return to the United States, if only to recoup some of the sleep and nourishment I'd missed out on. After a very invigorating, once-in-a-lifetime trip, I trekked to the airport to begin my journey home.

The first leg of my twenty-two-hour flight home was from Delhi, India to Istanbul, Turkey. It left India at four fifteen a.m., so I didn't bother to even attempt to go to bed the night before. My classmates and I enjoyed our last night dinner at a gorgeous restaurant in Delhi, and I returned to our hotel with just enough time to shower and catch my cab to head to the airport.

One of the most memorable things about India were the hundreds of wild animals that roamed the streets, cities, and monuments. Unlike the United States, where animals are contained in zoos or viewed as pets, the wildlife were considered to be an everyday part of life. They didn't bother people or stop the flow of traffic. I ran into my favorite wild animal – almost literally, mind you – on the way to the airport for my flight home. As the cab driver zoomed along the highway, right beside our car was a massive gray elephant, charging down the road.

I glanced up at it in awe of its vast size and presence; it was the most unique cab ride I'd ever experienced. The driver chuckled at my amazement of the animal and continued on to the airport. I gathered my belongings and buzzed through security to get to my gate.

To be honest, I don't even remember the first eight-hour flight that landed me in Istanbul. I was so unbelievably fatigued that the mindless motions of my flight became nothing more than a robotic routine. I remember lying in the airport, waiting for my flight and nodding off into Dreamland every few minutes. A loud announcement over the intercom would jolt me awake, and I would sleepily lift my head.

My flight was still on time, but boarding had not begun. Finally, the airline employee called our boarding section, and I stepped on the plane. I'm 99 percent sure that I spent the majority of that first leg of the flight sleeping, because I don't remember eating anything or even speaking with anyone. I was way too drained to care.

Obviously, the snoozing that my body automatically induced on the first flight was helpful, if not absolutely necessary. After the plane landed in Istanbul, I had to navigate my way through the terminals and find my connection flight. By the time I switched airplanes in Istanbul, I was much more conscious of my surroundings.

Traversing through an airport where the primary language of everyone was Turkish was quite difficult. It took me many questions, interpretations of symbols on signage, turnarounds, and backtracking before I figured out where I was supposed to be. Finally, after a long trek through the terminals and security, I arrived at my gate.

Similar to any other flight, I stood in line and surveyed the other passengers who'd be sharing the next fourteen hours of my life with me. I ended up chatting with two gentlemen behind me who raved about Dubai, a country I had not been to. I specifically remember being intrigued about the Dubai ATMs that spat out gold bars as a form of currency.

I couldn't even fathom that, presuming that gold bars were only good in videogames and board games. It seemed like some kind of urban legend or a daydream, but then the gentlemen started talking about a familiar place that was near and dear to my heart: Chicago. They joked about what a great experience they'd had there, but they were looking forward to returning to

Traveling the world with my trusted backpack

their homes in the States. I couldn't have agreed more.

The airline attendant started calling the first boarding groups to make their way toward the terminal entrance. All the passengers stockpiled in the area and ended up waiting in line for an extended period of time. The plane was slightly delayed, but once our tickets were scanned, the massive hordes of people were escorted down four flights of stairs, all balancing many pounds of luggage. We were then bussed like cattle out to the tarmac and up to the jumbo jet.

Squished in between stinky strangers and bulging luggage, I was an unhappy, tired camper on the bus. Various smells wafted from too many people in a confined space. I wanted to sit down, relax, and start the countdown for the twelve-hour extravaganza in the air toward home. Little did I know that our extended plane ride was going to be anything but relaxing.

I was shuffled, along with my fellow passengers, to the back of the plane to be seated in the lovely confines of economy coach seating. The airplane was huge. There were two seats on both sides, with an aisle in between, and five seats in the middle of the two aisles. People from all walks of life were piling into the plane and finding their assigned seats. I finally made my way to my seat, near the window on the left side of the airplane. I stuffed my belongings under the seat in front of me and settled into my temporary space.

I took note of everyone and everything going on around me. I've always been an exceedingly perceptive person, and this trait is heightened anytime I step foot on an airplane, where I am overly aware of my surroundings. This vigilance stems back to the memories of the historical accounts of September 11, 2001.

It's very difficult to ever forget (or even temporarily disregard for the duration of a short flight) the impact the terrorists had on the United States and the thousands of people who lost their lives that day. I was only fourteen years old at the time, but I will never forget the exact moment when I saw those first images of the World Trade Center collapse.

I gawked at the TV in horror; it was the epitome of devastation. Thousands of innocent people lost their family members, friends, and loved ones in a split second when a completely selfish act of terrorism struck a group of passengers. Unfortunately, each and every time I get on an airplane, my body triggers a subtle reminder in the back of my mind about that day.

I don't think the majority of people are as observant

as I am about their surroundings. There was a Turkish family sitting across from me in the middle seating area. One mother was tending to four children, who were all bombarding her with questions. The mother was overly concerned with getting her children's seatbelts fastened, which was a good thing. She frantically dug through her bag and pulled out games, stuffed animals, graham crackers, and any other security-cleared object that might serve to distract her little ones for a long time.

The plane began to fill up quickly, and I wondered who would be sitting in the seat that accompanied mine. Suddenly, I got my answer. A man in a red striped polo shirt and dress pants shuffled his carryon items in the overhead compartment over the aisle where I was sitting. He had dark, stiff hair and a rather manicured, dark black mustache. His skin had an olive twinge to it, and something about him gave the impression that he was some kind of businessman.

As soon as he took his seat, he immediately took his cell phone out of his pocket and began vigorously chatting with someone on the other line. I was unsure what language he was speaking, and I had no idea what he was talking about. I was exhausted, and at that point of the flight, I really didn't care. The man, who I will refer to as "Ira," invoked an overwhelming feeling of uneasiness in me for the duration of the flight.

The flight attendants began their spiel about the safety concerns and emergency procedures. As a seasoned veteran in aviation, I had no need for the A+ Airlines routine, so I leaned my head back on the rigid airplane pillow, hoping to find comfort in the miniscule amount of space I'd rented for the commute. I tuned out the overhead message that pulsated through the speaker system.

Just as I was about to head back to the Land of Snooze, I noticed something odd about my seatmate: He was really quite obviously nervous, and even after the flight crew asked everyone to turn off all cell phones, he continued to talk on his. With the massive amount of moving parts all over the airplane, it was nearly impossible for him to be pinpointed specifically for disobeying the rules.

Ira eventually complied and turned off his phone, but then he began to fidget with every item within his reach as the plan began taxiing to the runway. He took his belongings out of the seat pocket in front of him, then put them back – a process he repeated at least three times, like the instructions on the back of a shampoo bottle that no one pays attention to. He actually stood up while the plane was moving to adjust one of the large bags he'd stored in the overhead compartment.

It is well known that getting up anytime the seatbelt sign is illuminated is strictly prohibited, but he seemed unaware of that universal rule. He moved his head vigorously back and forth, looking around at everyone sitting around us. I noticed how perturbed his demeanor was and chalked it up to his nervousness about the flight.

While Ira was causing a rather subdued ruckus, I peered out the small window to the outside world. I was so happy to be returning home. Only another twelve hours. The engines began to rev, and the plane generated a massive amount of torque to lift us off the ground. We pummeled down the runway, and before I knew it, we were airborne.

We began a very steep ascent up to the high cruising altitude that the pilots had predetermined for our flight. Almost immediately after we departed from the ground, Ira jolted out of his seat, grabbed one of the bags full of items from the seat in front of him, and headed toward the back of the plane. He entered the restroom and slammed the door behind him.

Typically, no one is permitted to get up until clearance is given from the pilot that the plane has reached a safe altitude, so I was shocked and almost in disbelief that Ira decided he could do as he pleased. I also wondered what could be so urgent that would require him to leave his seat so quickly after takeoff. I was unsure whether anyone else around me thought it strange, but I didn't bother asking anyone their opinion.

Ira returned to his seat within five minutes, his ensemble changed from head to toe. Instead of the business casual attire he'd worn onto the plane, he was now garbed in a flowing, floral, button-down shirt, dark jeans and tan boat shoes, as if he were headed to a luau. *But in Chicago?* I wondered. The oddest part of his outfit was a multicolored fanny pack that looked like it was straight out of the 1980s. *What could he possibly have in that thing?* I was dying to know. None of the grown men I know wear fanny packs, and clearly, there was a reason for Ira's odd makeover.

His transformation from businessman to beach bum not only surprised me, but it actually made me nervous. This complete wardrobe change was unusual behavior for an airplane passenger. When he returned to his seat, his nervousness was even more apparent. He was twitching, and his knee moved up and down uncontrollably. Although it didn't directly imply that anything was amiss, I had never witnessed such odd conduct in the past. It was far different than a passenger just being nervous to fly.

The flight attendants began milling around in the cabin. They walked row by row, pushing the drink cart in front of them. When one of them approached us, I politely thanked her for the hospitality but chose not to get a drink. Unlike me, he ordered three whiskey-and-dark-soda drinks and instructed the flight attendant to "keep them coming." As Ira was served his initial drinks, our small compartmental area began to smell like the local bar after a night of binge drinking. The distinct stench of whiskey filled the air. He chugged one of the drinks down and immediately starting sipping the next one.

Very soon after the drinks were served, the flight attendants came around to deliver the first of a few meals that would be served on the flight. The airline surpassed my expectations two times over with the assortment of food they served. Since most domestic flights do not serve entire meals anymore, I recalled airplane food from when I was a kid. Back then, passengers were often given the choice of chicken, fish, or vegetarian meals. Unfortunately, the alleged meat portions never resembled actual chicken or fish, so the vegetarian meal was usually the safest bet: a mixture of noodles and vegetables in some kind of edible sauce. The food was always mildly warmed and barely passable for substantial intake of nutrition.

Having prepared myself for such a lackluster meal, I was delightfully surprised when I received an arrangement of hummus and pita, a real grilled chicken breast, a buttery, soft roll, a pile of gourmet green and black olives, and steamed, seasoned vegetables. The blend of wholesome food with palatable flavors was exceptionally appetizing. I dived into the food, but after a few short bites, I'd had enough. The long haul of travel was overwhelming and had negatively impacted my appetite.

At that point in the trip, an overstuffed stomach was the last thing I needed. So, instead of consuming the impressive offering of food, I put my head back and snuggled into the space between the window and the edge of the seat. I covered my eyes with a sleeping mask and tried to relax. I must have dozed off for about twenty minutes, but I suddenly had the urge to open my eyes, and what I saw was absolutely flabbergasting.

Every last bit of the relatively decadent food on my plate was gone*, as if a magical vacuum had come and sucked up every last left-over edible crumb. Dumbfounded by this, I turned to my right and saw Ira sitting there like the cat who'd quite literally swallowed the canary, silent and full of food. He was still slowly sipping his whiskey concoction and did not look at me. *Did this completely strange stranger just eat all the food off of my tray?* I wondered, aghast.

After gathering my thoughts, I concluded that he'd helped himself to my neglected feast. This left me with a very uneasy feeling, as if my privacy – what little I had in such close quarters with strangers – had been vandalized. I wondered, *if he had the audacity to eat my food while I was sleeping, what else will he do*

---

* The term "plate" is used very loosely here. For anyone who has been served a meal on an airplane, you know that they usually have some form of a hybrid tray to present all of the food in one removable manner. There are separate compartments to keep the different foods from touching one another. This so-called plate was such a platter.

during the trip? He refused to look over at me as I pulled it all together in my mind. I assumed he had hoped I wouldn't wake up until the trays, and therefore the evidence of his indiscretion, were removed by the flight attendants. It was one of the strangest things I'd ever experienced on a flight – at least up until that point.

I was already uncomfortable with my seatmate's odd and unnerving antiques, and we were only halfway through the flight. I wondered if anyone else had noticed Ira's strange behavioral patterns, but the other passengers seemed consumed with themselves and their own thoughts or destinations or schedules. It was as if I was the only one who noticed or even cared.

Little did I know that the scariest part of the trip had yet to occur. As we continued on, I tried to ignore Ira to make myself more comfortable. At one point, I looked over at him and noticed that he was making odd gestures toward another gentleman who was sitting about fifteen rows ahead of us, giving signals like a third-base coach or catcher in a baseball game. He put his hand up to his head, pulled on his ears, and thrashed his hands across his face. He then pointed in different directions and winked his eyes while moving his hands around.

Once again, I had no idea what he was doing, until I looked up toward the front of the airplane. The other man was clearly communicating with him with that same odd sign language. I had no idea what messages they were silently sending to one another, but it gave me a sick feeling in the pit of my stomach. I was instantaneously reminded of the attacks on our country.

When the horrific tragedies of 9/11 occurred, I couldn't help but follow the media as they attempted to explain the various pieces of the puzzle. The propaganda, news reports, and gruesome photos that plastered the television and Internet were heart-wrenching. The impact those terrorists had on the United States of America that unforgettable day is immeasurable. Even on that flight, some ten years later, I couldn't help but fear that it could happen again.

That horror encouraged me to think of the situation and take a step back to equate just how impactful September 11 really was. Because I'm an economist, I can't help but look at the whole sordid scenario through an economic lens. There was an undeniable, significant, measureable impact; those attacks changed the world. Aside from the tragic loss of lives that the country experienced during the actual attacks, the impression that those attacks left on the air traffic and travel industries are colossal. A quantifiable number of hours is devoted every year to the changes and updated protocols and security measures, all resulting from the attacks. To put this into perspective, I pulled some data from the United States Department of Transportation.

According to the Transportation Security Administration (TSA), the average amount of time it took for an individual to pass through security in 2010 was 8 minutes and 50 seconds. The Bureau of Transportation Statistics reported that in 2010, 629,521,640 domestic passengers went through standard security. What does this mean? It equates to 92,679,574 hours spent migrating through security in just one year. Consider what it means in terms of man-hours that could be used for labor or leisure, and you'll realize the costs are outstanding!

To create a valid comparison of what this number of hours entails, I will put it into another perspective. Approximately 44,557 people could be employed full time for a year, working an annual 2,080 hours in place of all that time spent milling through security, and that was only for one year, and only one of the many changes that were made as a result of 9/11. Almost 45,000 jobs were taken away in time alone due to additional security requirements, an astounding number of lost opportunities for employment in a time when everyone's bank account and personal economy could use a boost.

In addition, Americans have spent millions of dollars on "travel safe" bottles of shampoo, toothpaste, soap, deodorant, and other personal cleansing products, due to the change in size regulations. These overpriced items are just frivolous afterthoughts and do not account for the overwhelming amount of infrastructure invested in new security checkpoints in airports throughout the United States. The overall financial and economic impact was immeasurable.

Another form of time and energy spent for the attacks were the hundreds of media snapshots that highlighted and depicted the story. The motion picture *United 93* depicted a reenactment of the flight pattern and the terrorists' actions when they took that particular plane down. In the film, the terrorists signaled one another when the attacks were to occur. My situation with Ira, therefore, seemed all too familiar. Although the people in the movie were just actors, the desolation of the situation gave it an all-too-realistic vibe, and since those actors were using the same odd, silent way of communication, I couldn't help panicking when I saw Ira doing the same thing.

Sometimes in life, your gut feeling can be an excellent indication that you are in the midst of a bad situation*. Human instinct made me respond in the only way I knew how: I stared directly at Ira in such an overt manner that he knew I was noticing his strange behavior and sign language. I needed to give him a clear signal that I was not only watching the two of them, but I was also ready to act if it became necessary. I didn't really know what else to do, so I acted on a whim, at the spur of the very strange moment.

At that point, my actions were driven by fear. It was difficult to react to such a situation without the loyalty or participation of those around me. I was on an international flight. The people around me weren't prone to automatically thinking of terrorism aboard the flight. Their Towers and Pentagon had not been destroyed. It was the U.S. that was attacked, not them, and I'd only assumed the others would have harbored that same underlying fear and concern. I didn't know if anyone around me was American, and I felt completely alone in the world.

Before I could decide if I should talk to the flight

---

*   Chapter Sixteen offers a thorough explanation of the origination of my "gut feeling." It all began when I was a child, with my mother's worldly advice…

attendants to inform them of my observations, Ira stood up and walked over to linger by the bathroom. Almost instantaneously, his partner became mobile as well and made his way up near the galley area. They were chatting rather quickly in a language I didn't understand. They used a plethora of hand signals and movements while they heatedly, hurriedly discussed whatever it was they were talking about.

I didn't recall Ira getting on the plane with anyone, nor had I seen him talking to anyone before boarding the plane. For a split second, I kept an eagle-eyed stare on them, not daring to look away.

Five minutes later, which seemed like an eternity to me, their conversation was interrupted by a flight attendant who forcefully instructed both gentlemen to return to their seats. She reminded them that it was impermissible to gather near the front of the aircraft, due to safety regulations.

Like scolded schoolboys, they finished up with an exchange of a few more words and returned to their seats, though Ira immediately resumed his sign language from there.

My stomach sank again. I was so uncomfortable in his presence that I didn't want him to return to our row, but at least he had obeyed the flight attendant and didn't seem to be causing any other issues besides getting on my nerves.

The last leg of the flight was even more tense than the first part. I practically sat on the edge of my seat, anxiously waiting for more of Ira's peculiar behavior to ensue, anticipating that he'd do at least a few more odd things before we landed. Luckily, he remained relatively normal, though I couldn't keep my paranoid mind from conjuring up all sorts of potential evildoings.

Because my imagination insisted on running wild, the next few hours were grueling. Time crawled at a snail's pace as I anticipated all the worst-case scenarios. I really believed there was a chance of danger, and I just could not ignore my gut feeling.

By the time we reached Chicago, I was so thrilled to be home that I put my thoughts of him out of my mind. I shuffled through the crowd and bolted off the airplane as soon as it pulled into the gate. I stood in line at customs and chatted on my phone with my sister. It was so good to be back to the home of the brave, though I didn't really feel so brave at all. After a long wait for all of my fellow passengers, I was called to the customs desk. I hadn't purchased anything of real value in India, so it was a relatively smooth and quick transaction.

I had flown often by then, but until that flight, I'd never really thought my safety was in jeopardy. Despite the countless hours spent on safety checks and security measures, I felt as though something still could have happened. It was instinct, and I refused to tell myself that I was over-thinking it, even if I was half-asleep.

Originally, I'd headed halfway around the world to check an international class off the list of requirements for my master's degree. My educational venture to fly to a developing foreign country taught me a little more than I bargained for. I realized I am, in so many ways, a very small fish in a very massive pond, and the cultural differences, thoughts, and demeanor of people varies greatly between the countries they call home. While my suspicions turned out to be unfounded, I do not regret trusting my intuition on the airplane with Ira. It felt natural.

It was *my* cultural differences that reared me to have that intuition. Every time I get on a plane, I can't help but remember the shocking attacks that frame my mindset. Every day, we live our lives based on what we've learned and experienced and seen and heard in the past. Like so many others, I lived through the tragedy of September 2011, and I cannot stop my uneasiness for strange behavior on an airplane now, nor will I ever be able to do so. The memories of those falling Towers will forever plague me because something that severe can never be forgotten – and maybe shouldn't.

That was one leg on my journey as a passenger on A+ Airlines, and just like all the others, it was its own unique adventure, as unnerving as it was. I felt compelled to include the story of Ira to demonstrate how much the world has changed, even in my own short lifetime. The airline industry was forever reformed after September 11, 2001. It is necessary to be aware of your surroundings and speak up if something seems amiss. Ira made me feel as though I was in danger, and – right or wrong – I couldn't shake the stigma, fearing that something negative was bound to occur on that flight. This is something that might never change for Americans or for me.

After thinking about Ira's actions that day, I gained another perspective on his intentions. Since I lived to tell you this story, the man obviously did not commit a terrorist act on or with that airplane. I've concluded that Ira was a watchdog.

His actions on the plane were undeniably odd, but I am now convinced that Ira could have been a scout, seeing how far one can push their luck in an airborne vessel. He wanted to determine exactly how much he could get away with, how many paranoid buttons he could push and rules he could break before someone noticed. From my perspective, no one paid enough attention to his strange behavior. It took the flight attendants a while to notice him standing near the airplane bathroom that was clearly marked as restricted.

I promised that each of my stories would be impactful, and I can say with 100 percent certainty that this particular experience made a lasting impression on me. I will never forget how that weird man looked or how he made me feel. I seemed to be the only one who noticed or cared about his weird behavior, but for the sake of my fellow travelers' sanity and security, I'm glad the entire fiasco was not blown up into a bigger spectacle than it should have been. Fortunately, it was an isolated incident, and I haven't experienced anything like it since, but it was a flight I'll never forget.

Chapter Four

Mandy, the Inspirational Model

My job required me to travel each week to cities to meet with my customers. On this particular journey, we breezed through our meeting quicker than anticipated and zoomed to the airport to catch a flight home.

I arrived at the airport in Minneapolis, Minnesota, about two hours earlier than my scheduled flight. I frantically raced around to return the oversized vehicle I'd been driving in the Great White North. I grabbed my carryon luggage and zoomed over to the desk at A+ Airlines. My original flight was not supposed to leave for three to four more hours, but I was itching to get home.

I approached the counter and whipped out my boarding pass to hand it to the A+ Airlines employee, pleading with her to grant me access to the earlier flight. Luckily, there was an open seat, and I jumped at the chance to get home a few hours early. I yanked my ticket from her hand and skidded over to security.

Lucky for me, the airport was relatively small, which meant a quick scoot through security. After my identification and boarding pass were approved, I got in line behind a businessman.

As soon as some of the counter space was vacant, I grabbed three large bins. I unpacked my laptop computer and a small Ziploc bag full of liquid items and ripped my shoes off my feet. I sent my belongings over the conveyor belt and through the X-ray machines. The TSA agent scanned them and sent them through the other end. I shuffled through the metal detector. Once I reached the other side, I repacked my stuff and headed off to my gate.

When I arrived in the terminal, I double-checked the flight information on the header. I made it with about forty-five minutes to spare, so I settled into a comfortable chair beside a few of my would-be fellow passengers. I tore a book away from my luggage and opened it, but before I had time to focus my eyes and start reading, I inadvertently found myself eavesdropping on a conversation between a young woman and an older man next to me.

The woman was talking about her profession. She mentioned the terms "identity" and "image" and "self-esteem," and I was automatically tuned into their conversation. I had studied self-perception during my undergraduate work at Indiana University. My friends and I had spent hours discussing how people perceive themselves and what influences can cause an individual to make changes in themselves. Each person had their own opinion, differing from the unique upbringings and media influence that each of us endured.

Especially among young teen and adult women, self-image can be a major factor in a person's happiness. There are so many internal and external things that factor into it. Since this was a topic I was passionate about, my interest in their conversation was piqued immediately.

I began my conversation with the two people by saying something to the effect of, "Excuse me for interrupting, but I couldn't help but hear what you're talking about. Self-image is such a pressing issue in society right now. What exactly do you do? Oh, and by the way, my name is Kersten."

Initially, they seemed a bit taken aback by the abrupt

interlude into their conversation. Both individuals turned to look over to me and smiled. I might have been barging into their chat a bit forcefully, but I never gave that a second thought.

First, the man who was sitting in the chair connected to mine introduced himself as "Jim." He was a sixty-something salesman who'd been in the business for a long time. He had salt-and-pepper hair, freshly cut. He was from the Chicago suburbs, and that made him all the more interesting to me.

Jim said he sold dairy products, and I wanted to know more. He went on to tell me that his company was a major manufacturer of milk products specifically. He mentioned some of the large accounts they held, and by the well-known names of their partners, I could safely assume that the scope of the consumers he served covered approximately 90 percent of the country's milk consumption.

He explained his role in the sales force of the company, and I made reference to one of my fellow salespeople being in a similar line in a previous position. We mentioned names of people we knew and ultimately discovered that we had a mutual acquaintance. Talk about six degrees of dairy salespeople! What a small world it truly is! When Jim and I finished chatting about work-related nonsense, I turned to the young woman who sat in front of me.

She introduced herself as "Mandy," and she was a twenty-something young woman on her way to Chicago to speak at a self-identity seminar. She was dressed in modern, but plain attire. When I inquired further into her purpose for traveling to my homeland, she explained her story from the beginning. What had started with me, in effect, butting in was now a three-person discussion between Jim, Mandy, and me.

"I'm a former model," Mandy announced right away.

To be very honest, that would not have been my guess. Though she was an attractive young woman and well poised, she didn't fit the my stereotypical type-cast for a model; she was nothing like the ones I'd seen on television, in magazines, or on the Internet. I'd always envisioned models as extremely thin, tall, dainty young women with limited imperfections. Most of the photographs I've seen have been airbrushed to diminish any flaws that might be seen by the naked eye. Mandy was nothing like I imagined a model could be.

Of course, the whole concept of a model is almost deceiving in itself. I don't want to disregard the hard work that models put into their careers, so allow me to preface my dissection by saying I have the utmost respect for anyone who has a passion and sticks to it. The men and women who devote their lives to modeling put a great deal of effort into their appearances and their bodies, a dedication I cannot even fathom. I simply do not have that much self-control.

The image that these so-called models portray isn't much of a model at all for general society; their figures and looks are not achievable for the greater population. Nevertheless, these men and women devote their entire lives to creating an image that is desirable to the public. Some go to extreme measures to alter their body to fit that desirable look. Unfortunately, everyone has begun to hold models accountable to this mega-thin, airbrushed, almost unnatural perfection, and it is simply not reality for most human beings.

When I was in school, we discussed modeling and its impacts on today's society. Models tend to be so close to the "perfect"* woman that the term we used to discuss the image in class was "plastic." Prior to that discussion, I had never thought about any person as being plastic. The word refers to the moldable perfection that plastic can be turned into, just as models are considered to be flawless people.

Barbie, for example, is the prototypical plastic woman, both literally and figuratively. Barbie's dimensions and size are virtually unrealistic for a woman to achieve, yet little girls are

---

* "Perfect," when used to describe the physical appearance of people, is completely subjective. One of the most important things to remember is that perfection really is a matter of opinion. As the old adage goes, beauty is in the eye of the beholder.

given Barbie to play with. Her life is glamorized with gorgeous clothes, sparkly accessories, and an idealistic boyfriend named Ken, who is equally plastic. What more could any girl ask for? Many people strive to achieve the Barbie dream life, but unfortunately, it is not the norm.

Mandy, whom I met on the plane, was anything but plastic or perfect. She was simply average. She had long, flowing black hair and big blue eyes that beamed when she spoke passionately about her job. Of course I didn't dare ask her what size she wore, but she appeared to be close to a woman's Size Fourteen pants.

Her forehead bore a few wrinkles, and smile lines enclosed her mouth and eyes in permanent parentheses. She wore minimal makeup, plain black business clothing, and her hair tied up in a ponytail. In other words, if you had walked by Mandy on the street, you wouldn't have thought twice about her being anything but ordinary, based on the outer image she portrayed. The fact that she was a model would not immediately come to mind.

Mandy was just like any other woman, and I couldn't quite connect the dots between her occupation and the way she looked. I was intrigued by her former career, though, so I inquired more to find out exactly what she'd modeled and what she was doing now.

She started by asking both Jim and me if we were familiar with the Dove Campaign for Real Beauty. The mention of this campaign made her story click in my mind. I happily answered that I was familiar with it and that I thought it to be an inspiring work of advertisement. Jim was unaware of it, so Mandy described the campaign and her role in it.

The Dove Campaign for Real Beauty was an ongoing advertising scheme that challenged the norms for what society deems to be beautiful for women. The campaign questioned what real women look like versus that which has always been portrayed in the media. When they surveyed women around the world, the facilitators found that many women do not really believe they are beautiful.

According to the Dove Campaign website*, only 2 percent of surveyed women in 2004 described themselves as beautiful. Some based their self-judgment on what they saw as normal in the media. This was a detriment to self-esteem, which was already fairly low in some women. Because beauty is such a subjective concept, the company saw an opportunity to redefine what makes people "beautiful."

The company strived to create awareness that all women are beautiful. They used real, ordinary women, models who were comfortable in their own bodies, just the way they were. They depicted these women in their underwear on billboards, in television commercials, in magazine ads, and through online media – women of all shapes, sizes, ethnicities, ages, and curves. In doing so, the company defied the norm, exhibiting models who loved themselves just as they were. Not only did the ads promote self-appreciation, but also the use of Dove products to keep skin healthy and beautiful. In essence, it was a great marketing campaign.

The campaign received mixed reactions, however. Many women offered an overwhelmingly positive response to this campaign and saw it as liberal, courageous support for everyday women in their natural state. On the contrary, some viewers said they did not wish to see "chunky"** women flaunting their underwear on a billboard. This was a complete 180-degree turn from what consumers expected. They were used to the skinny, idealistic models trying to motivate them to purchase goods, and Dove was doing something different – something far more

---

* The website for the Dove Campaign for Real Beauty can provide additional information on the studies completed to determine these statistics. The website can be found at http://www.dove.us/Social-Mission/campaign-for-real-beauty.aspx.

** This was an actual word used in reports to describe how some people reacted to the campaign. This is not a personal word choice, as I would not select this word to describe anyone carrying a bit of excess weight.

real. The company chose to advertise to a different group of consumers and to connect on a whole new level.

Personally, I had to support a campaign like that. From a factual standpoint, I researched an article that reported some of the average sizes within the United States. *Plus Model Magazine* reported that the average plus-sized model is between Sizes Six and Fourteen.*** The website also reported that the average dress size of women in the United States is a Fourteen. In other words, models in standard advertisements are much smaller than the average consumer who will eventually be purchasing those clothes.

These statistics may be shocking, since most people view the perfectly thin, perfectly plastic models as the supposed norm. The campaign dispensed these assumptions. Being a woman, I would consider myself to have a biased opinion. I will also venture to say that I have much more sympathy for women and our self-image. I was fully supportive of the message that this bold political move sent.

After a detailed explanation, Mandy informed us that she was one of the models in the campaign. She described her firsthand experience and explained how she felt about her own body and physical appearance. She wanted to liberate people of all sizes, men and women alike to feel comfortable loving their bodies in a happy, healthy manner.

She was photographed in her underwear as one of the "real women" of the world. Her photos were posted in magazines, on billboards in major cities, and on the Internet as a marketing tool for Dove. After the campaign subsided, she was very inspired to work in the field of motivational speaking.

Mandy now traveled around the country as a motivational speaker at conferences for promoting self-worth and education on body image. She developed a program that deliberates the definition of beauty. Her presentations were centered on positive

***   *Plus Model Magazine* reported these statistics on their website at http://www.plus-model-mag.com/2012/01/plus-size-bodies-what-is-wrong-with-them-anyway/.

reinforcement of women's body images in any shape or size, regardless of what the stereotypical norm might be.

As she described her program in greater detail, I became more engaged in our conversation. I could not wait to hear how she worked to change the viewpoints of people throughout the country. All of a sudden, I interrupted her explanation and blurted out the one lingering thought in my head: "Do you tell people how wrong they are when they make negative comments about the women in the Dove Campaign being 'overweight' or 'flawed'?" I felt so passionate about the benefits of the program that I couldn't help but wonder. Many people who are close to me have gone through the pain of negative self-image, so her message really hit close to home.

I expected her to make a crude comment or retort about the negative feedback from the audience. I was sure Mandy was going to blurt out a few choice expletives to describe the actions and reactions of those people. In other words, I anticipated some form of disapproval for those who disagreed with the liberal form of advertising because that was what I would have done.

So, her answer genuinely surprised me: "I always try to focus on the positive when I speak with and to audiences. I don't really tell people they are wrong, but more that I have a differing opinion." She said she always tried to support her opinions with facts about the campaign and self-image in general. When people did offer negative reactions, Mandy framed her response with only positive verbiage to promote positivity. Her demeanor facilitated the rethinking of disagreement. When she was finished explaining this to me, I sat there nodding for a few seconds, to reassure her that I understood.

I took a few minutes to myself to reflect on what she was telling me. Not only was I impressed by her unrelenting optimism, I relished in her genuine delivery. If my interactions with others were so well orchestrated, I could communicate much more effectively with others. I wanted to mimic her actions in the future.

Her positive approach to such a sensitive subject is

very different than the one many would take. It is natural to go into defense mode when someone disagrees with or makes an argument or negative comment about an issue we care deeply about. People intrinsically support one side or another on most controversial topics. Hundreds, if not thousands, of factors can play into our opinions, and that makes it difficult to change the way others think.

In the case of the Dove campaign, most of the participants and individuals who formed it wanted to discuss positive perceptions and interpretations of it. The negative feedback from outsiders could have been a real point of contention for the models, even taken as an insult to them as individuals. Mandy's approach to take the adverse comments and turn them into something that could be discussed and supported was utterly ingenious.

Mandy focused solely on helping people understand the campaign and body image rather than negating it, and her plan worked. She told me that her public speaking gig had been very successful. Women, children, and men from all over the world had written to thank her for inspiring them to find beauty within themselves.

Those who attended her presentations were engaged, asking questions and taking notes when she brought up subjects with which they were unfamiliar. Her audiences all had different reactions to her presentations. Some of the people who were deeply influenced on an entirely larger level stayed in contact with her for a prolonged period of time after the fact. They were changed forever by her message.

Mandy was booked through the next few months, having to travel to a different city every week. This was a financial testimonial of how impactful her work and speeches were. She was queued up for our flight to Chicago to head home after her presentation in Minneapolis.

After she explained all of this to me, I sat there in utter amazement, thoroughly impressed. After talking with Mandy, I believe much of the success could be attributed to her efforts to create a positive learning environment for her patrons. Her outlook on body image was to question what people said and how they viewed self-worth rather than telling them what was right or wrong. Everyone's opinion is different, as beauty is truly in the eye of the beholder.

Our conversation persisted until the A+ Airline employee called us to start the boarding process. We discussed the possibility of the three of us sitting near one another on the airplane. Due to the number of passengers who boarded before me, the last form of communication I had with Mandy was a passing smile as I headed toward the rear of the plane.

Although it was brief, my conversation with Jim and Mandy left me with more questions than answers. It caused me to think about both the Dove Campaign and how body image directly affects people every day. The campaign was a bold statement for the company.

It encouraged people of all body types to highlight their unique attributes and feel comfortable in their own skin. On some, it had a negative effect. After speaking with Mandy, though, I no longer felt any angst toward those who disagreed with the message. I can appreciate that some have a differing opinion than mine.

Mandy was an amazing woman, able to connect with people on a different level by getting them to communicate, think, and develop more positive opinions. Her strategy certainly worked on me, and I was thoroughly convinced.

Positivity has such a great impact on those who exert it. From Mandy's recollections, I learned a lot about myself, how I interact with others, and different ways to conduct myself. I vowed to at least consider incorporating positivity into my reactions in the future. The strategy had worked for her, and she was the expert!

We never know what we might learn from a person, and the possibilities are endless. I will never forget the valuable lesson that Mandy taught me just by being her natural self. I also never truly appreciated true beauty until I met her. She was the epitome of it. My flights continued, but this was a lesson that stuck with me long after that parting smile.

Chapter Five

Harry, the Most Humble Football Fan

I visited southern California for a business trip just before Christmas one year. Being a Chicago native, I am used to a brisk, chilly winter with lots of white, fluffy snow to characterize the holidays. The smell of pine trees being cut down fills the air. The traditions are endless. My friends and I visit the German Fest off State Street to sip on homemade glug to keep us warm during the cold, dreary season. My mother bakes a slew of scrumptious holiday cookies that fills the house with a sugary aroma. My favorite ham, covered with gingersnap cookie crumbs, brown sugar, and Dijon mustard, is always delicious. There are so many things to enjoy during that festive time of year.

It was the first time I'd ever traveled so close to Christmas day, and the dry heat and sandy beaches of southern Cali did not feel quite right for Christmastime. I was anxious to get back home after a long week of hard work. The first leg of my flight took me from Orange County to Las Vegas, Nevada. From there, I'd fly nonstop to Chicago. Finally, I was going to start my journey back home.

The flight was absolutely packed. Ever the early bird,

though, I made it onto the airplane as one of the first passengers and took a seat toward the front. I chose the window seat just in case my book got too boring; at least I'd have something to look at. I settled down in my seat, placed my carryon bag under the seat in front of me, and waited impatiently to see who would join me in the row.

A man, around twenty-nine or thirty, asked me if the aisle seat was taken. I told him it wasn't, and he quietly sat down. He had a muscular build and jet-black hair with a scruffy beard in a matching color. His complexion was olive, complemented perfectly by his dark brown eyes. He was quite large in size and reminded me somewhat of a Chicago Bears linebacker. We didn't exchange further words until the third part of our entourage joined our row.

The third man's name was "Nelson." Unlike the other gentlemen, he had a petite build for a man, and there was only a bit of reddish, short hair on his semi-balding head. He was dressed in worn-out jeans and a polo shirt. Nelson stood beside the row with a grin as wide as a semi-truck on his face. He chuckled a bit to himself, looked over at the burly man sitting in the aisle seat, and began shuffling through his belongings in his pocket.

What is he looking for?

He took out a money clip filled with a variety of denominations of bills and attempted to bribe the man out of his seat. He was obviously a businessman, a negotiator, at heart and knew exactly what he wanted. He ranted briefly about how he absolutely despised sitting in the middle seat, then offered to give the other gentleman twenty-five dollars to move over and give him the aisle seat.

The burly man and I looked at each other with a bit of confusion on our faces, but then he shook Nelson's hand and agreed to the deal.

I had never seen such a negotiation take place over an airline seat before, an unspoken contract for subletting an aisle seat. I guess I understood where Nelson was coming from. The flight would be a solid three hours and fifty-five minutes, and the middle seat was extremely uncomfortable.

The middle passenger has to sit between two others who ultimately reigns over the armrests on either side. The space in front of the seat is limited to a few inches. If the person in front of the unfortunate middle-seat passenger decides to recline even a few centimeters, the distance seems like miles. It is virtually impossible to turn to one's right or left when sitting in that position, so the only movement is a bit of space directly in front. I wasn't quite sure why he glanced my way before making his decision to move. I assumed he wanted to make sure I was someone he could stand sitting in close proximity with for the next few hours.

As he moved toward me, the burly man took that opportunity to introduce himself as "Harry." As he got comfortable in his seat, he turned to me and offered half of the money Nelson had given him. I was initially confused by this and slightly uncomfortable about it. I refused to take it and turned my head away, telling him I didn't want it and giggling out of sheer nervousness at the man's odd behavior. He insisted that it was only fair since I now had to sit by him for the next few hours, and that only made me wonder what I was really in for. I felt more than a little awkward taking the money from him, but since he insisted, I quickly put it in my carryon bag and forgot about it. He shook my hand and finished moving his belongings to the inside seat.

As our fellow passengers were fighting their way down the space-restricted aisle to find their seats, my male row mates started up a conversation about their reasons for being in Las Vegas. Both had been in the city on business for the entire week. As different as they were from a physical standpoint, there were some commonalities between them. They actually worked in similar fields and knew quite a few of the same people. I tuned out of their conversation when the name-dropping of their mutual acquaintances began. Clearly, they were indirectly connected through their network, and I was not part of that web.

Once they had mulled over the plethora of mutual acquaintances in their respective industries, they inquired about my occupation and why I'd been in Sin City. I smiled and began telling them what I did for a living and why I'd ended up in the middle of the desert.

I gave them my "elevator speech,"* as I learned it to be called in business school. I can still hear my professors emphasizing the importance of capturing that first thirty seconds of someone's attention: "You have a brief window of opportunity, and if you don't capture their interest, you won't be asked to come in for an interview." The professors were accurate with their assumptions under most circumstances, but I used my prepared speech all too often. It was almost like a recording, with very little variation or inflection in my vocal tones. Although I wasn't trying to score an interview with either of those two gentlemen, there was only so much I wanted to reveal in my initial introduction to Nelson and Harry.

I disclosed some basic information: where I lived, what I did for a living, the hobbies I enjoyed, and that I am the author of an economics book. As I mentioned where I was living at the time, Nelson's demeanor perked up, and he chimed in to let me know we were practically neighbors. Coincidentally, he only lived minutes away from me, and we unknowingly shared a bike path that I ran on quite frequently. He used to walk his dogs on the same path in the evenings. I would venture to say with confidence that at some point, I probably passed him while racing into the sunset, unaware that I would ever meet the man while sitting on a plane from Las Vegas.

Next, I steered the conversation toward one of my favorite

---

* An "elevator speech," as I learned in school, is the thirty-second blurb a person has the opportunity to share in order to pique the interest of a perspective employer. The reference comes from the idea that if you get caught in an elevator with a potential business contact, you need to dazzle them quickly, because the time on the elevator is limited. If you don't gain someone's attention initially, they won't be inclined to contact you for a position.

topics: Chicago's sports teams. My love for the Chicago Bears seemed to be a safe segue into a new conversation since one of my seat-mates was from Chicago, and the other one looked like he could have played for the NFL. They nodded in approval of the team and agreed that they were avid fans as well. We turned our attention from end zones to home plate and bantered back and forth a bit about the cross-town rivalry between the Cubs and the Sox. Since we were at the cusp of a new season, it was a timely subject. The Blackhawks were mentioned a few times as we, and we all reveled in the memory of winning the Stanley Cup just a few years prior.

Somehow, our conversation morphed from athletics to Chicago-style cuisine. The three of us conversed back and forth about some of Harry's favorite hidden dives, where they allegedly served the best burritos, authentic Mexican food, Italian cuisine, Chicago-style pizzas, and a variety of other types of delectable Windy City treats and eats.

We reveled in the glory of our shared hometown, our kind of town for sure, and how loyal the three of us were to the area. Our conversation was boisterous and booming as the jet engines roared for takeoff. The flight attendants announced our clearance for departure, and the commencement of our almost four-hour airplane ride began.

Normally, I would have dreaded such a lengthy domestic, as I've never been one who's found it easy to sit still. Fortunately for me, the two men sitting next to me on that flight were an absolute delight to chat with, and the time flew by (you can decide if the pun is intended or not!). I learned about each of their families, their occupations, hopes, dreams, goals, ambitions, and the commonalities between us.

Both of them were hardworking, devoted fathers who loved their children more than anything else. They were happy to go to work to provide the best life they could imagine for their kids. They bragged about the accomplishments and awards their kids won, just as any proud parent would. I admired their sincerity when they spoke about their children.

Nelson complained of his harsh, heart-breaking divorce and suggested that I avoid marriage at all costs. Since I was significantly younger than him, I assumed it was a case of his fatherly instincts kicking in; he felt as if it was his duty to warn me of the pitfalls of walking down the aisle. His intentions were sincere, and he struck me as a loyal individual. His zest for life was focused solely on the happiness of his children and his personal success in the business he owned.

I shared a common interest with Nelson in that his daughter was enrolled as a college sophomore at Indiana University, my alma mater. As a devout Hoosier fan and lover of the school, I gleamed at the chance to talk about how wonderful the town, people, faculty, and the school itself are. I reminisced about my experiences on campus, somewhat daydreaming of the excitement and unexpected fun that was a constant during my college days. He grinned and implied that his daughter, from what little she shared with him, was in the midst of a similar experience. Her major carried some similarities to mine, and he was elated – if not a bit relieved – to hear such positive feedback from an alumnus.

As I picked up cues about both of their personalities, I realized how exceptionally humble Harry was. Whenever Nelson made an off-color comment or negative remark, Harry leaned over to me and whispered his disagreement. The big man was not shy or quiet, but the way he spoke about himself and others was quite different.

He downplayed much of his success, and from what I can remember, he really didn't offer up additional information about himself. He was confident and poised as a manager at his company, but his hard work and dedication was conveyed with humility and grace. One would never guess that he was harboring such a lofty secret that I would later learn.

Harry's offering of the money made much more sense after I got to know him a bit. It was intrinsically within his nature to cater to others around him and share whatever he earned. It wasn't that he felt bad or obligated to give me the money; he actually *wanted* to. I was a complete stranger to him, yet he shared his earnings with me. His actions spoke louder than his words, and that small act of generosity was a mere foreshadowing of what I would come to learn about the man sitting next to me.

We continued to muse on a variety of topics to pass the time. Some of them interested me more than others. At points, I checked out the view over the mountains, spotting the rocky, rugged terrain that passed swiftly below the aircraft. I followed the clouds with my eyes and lost myself in the trance of the gorgeous scenery.

I tuned out parts of the conversation, just as I'm sure each one of them did as well, then keyed back in when I heard anything that intrigued me. The conversation continued relatively steadily until we were instructed to prepare for final descent into Chicago's Midway Airport.

The three of us locked our tray tables in front of us and handed whatever was left of our plastic drink cups and napkins over to the flight attendant for proper disposal. As we prepared to land, Nelson fished through his pockets once again and pulled out his business card. He handed one to me and one to Harry and generically told us to keep in touch. Following his lead, I rummaged through my carryon bag to find one to distribute to each of them. I clenched my hand on two cards and forked them over to each of the men.

Personally, I've always considered the handing out of business cards on airplanes to be an awkward follow-up to the end of a flight. The majority of the time, neither party has any intention to make contact with the other post-flight. It is somewhat of an unspoken rule that although it is a hospitable gesture to exchange contact information, the chances of ever communicating again are slim to none. Luckily, there are always exceptions to the rule.

We scooted out of the airplane in record time, and I found myself scurrying to the bus that would take me to the parking lot where my car was stashed. The last thing I wanted to do was linger around the gate reiterating how nice it was to meet someone. I'd been gone for nearly an entire week, and I was ready to return home for some much-needed rest and relaxation. Since it was a Friday afternoon, I anxiously turned my cell phone off and welcomed the start of my weekend.

On the drive into the office on Monday morning, I powered up my cell phone and heard it beep a few times. when I looked at the phone, I realized I'd missed a phone call and a voicemail over the weekend. When I called into the voicemail to see who it was, I heard an unfamiliar male voice on the other end.

Nelson awkwardly stumbled over several of his words before he managed to ask me to meet up with his daughter to discuss the endless opportunities at Indiana University. It was endearing that he trusted me to answer his daughter's questions about her future, and since he'd gone to such lengths to make an effort to help his daughter get more out of her education, I agreed to meet both of them for lunch. It was an unexpected phone call, but both of them were exceptionally grateful when I accepted their invitation.

We met the following week, while his daughter was on a break from school. It was a short, but productive lunch, and I offered her some of the best tips I could – information I'd have appreciated as a young student at a massive university. Only a veteran of the school could really provide the best insights, tricks, and secrets.

I talked with her about building a proper résumé and told her which offices she should visit and who she should meet with, since I remembered some of the most brilliant people – staff members who had the connections to introduce students to the vast network of internship and job opportunities.

From her reaction, I think Nelson's daughter was slightly overwhelmed with the cram session of knowledge I spewed at her. In only an hour, over lunch, I crammed approximately three to four hours' worth of information in for her. I wanted to tell her as much as I could before I needed to get back to the office.

Just before I left, Nelson asked if I'd heard from Harry

yet, and I noncommittally responded that I hadn't; I really never expected to hear from either one of them. He chuckled to his daughter and nudged her toward the door of the restaurant. They each thanked me for my help and waved goodbye when we parted ways.

Three months passed, and out of the blue, I received an e-mail one afternoon from Harry on my computer at work. I captured the name with my eyes, but one of my clients at that time had a very similar name, and for some reason or another, I assumed the message was from that client. I opened the e-mail to find a lengthy message, beginning with an apology for losing the business card I'd given to him.

He mentioned that he'd just found it and had decided to write me a message. It was just after the holiday season, and I had been swamped with family engagements, gift-giving, and ringing in the New Year with my friends and family. I never expected to hear from him again, so it was a treat to receive his e-mail after a few months.

The craziness of the holiday season is contagious, and Harry had a similarly busy schedule. He asked me a few follow-up questions regarding some of the items we'd discussed on the airplane. He said he'd been traveling quite a bit, and since domestic and international travel is one of my favorite hobbies, my response mostly centered on that. I asked him where he'd been and what he'd been up to in those places. Since I didn't know the man beyond a three-hour phone conversation on an airplane, I found it difficult to make small talk via e-mail. Still, I shot off the best response I could and continued with my work.

Within twenty-four hours, I had a response from Harry with shocking news, explaining that all of his travel and busyness over the last three months was because his brother had just won the Super Bowl. At first, I was thoroughly confused, so I went back and reread his message at least four times. I couldn't believe what I was reading.

His brother was one of the starting offensive linemen for one of the best teams in the National Football League. He played for the Jacksonville Jackhammers.* His team was awarded one of the most prestigious denominations as the world champions of American football. Being the avid Chicago Bears fan that I am, I was absolutely shocked at this news. I viewed the Chicago Bears players as heroes, and I'd looked up to the team ever since childhood. I never dreamt of knowing someone even remotely connected to the NFL, let alone the relative of a Super Bowl champion.

I'm admittedly nosy and inquisitive, so I checked out his brother's profile on the Jacksonville Jackhammers website and was awestruck when I saw his picture. The brothers looked nearly identical. *How could Harry not have told us about his brother's success in the NFL when we were discussing sports on our flight?* I wondered.

Harry was overtly proud of his brother, and his happiness came through even in an e-mail. I was a bit confused as to how such a successful, wealthy man such as Harry would ever end up sitting next to me on A+ Airlines. His demeanor was no different from anyone else's. I figured someone so closely related to an NFL superstar would have a different attitude.**

Later in his e-mail, he asked me to meet him at one of his favorite local restaurants for lunch, so we could catch up and chat about my first book. I was completely dumbfounded that such a man would be even remotely interested in knowing more

---

* Anyone who follows the National Football League (NFL) knows that the Jacksonville Jackhammers is a fictional team that I made up. For the sake of Harry and his brother's privacy and anonymity, I have opted to avoid providing any specific information that might reveal his or his brother's identity. One of the most endearing personal characteristics about Harry was his humility, and I would never want to compromise that trait.

** I judged the gracious attitude that someone of his status would have. Because I've always grown up thinking of the hard-working NFL players as heroes, I could not fathom even the thought of knowing someone of that level of success. I would categorize this as being star struck.

about *my* book, particularly since it was about economics. *Won't he only want to talk about football?*

Nevertheless, when I met Harry for lunch, he was just as courteous and humble as he was when he'd sat next to me on the airplane. I was nervous to rendezvous with him, now that I knew much more about his personal life, but he was the same old Harry I'd known on the plain, complete with that wonderful, unassuming personality. We talked about business, our jobs, his children, and my book.

I briefly asked him what it felt like to be the brother of a world champion. He laughed and told me he still thought of his brother as just an ordinary guy, the kid who wrestled around with him at home when they were young. He told me that despite what his brother had achieved in adulthood, they both knew how vitally important it was to remember their roots.

Harry thanked me for meeting him and shook my hand to say goodbye. He was just like everyone else and never gave me any indication that he regarded himself as superior in any way. He was sure to build his own reputation of success, exclusive to any of his family members or friends. He reminded me a few times that humility is a necessity in life.

Since that lunch, I have pondered his wise words over and over again. It is crucial to remember where we came from, and it's honorable to be humble. Harry's guidance has been an effective tool in my career and personal life since then. People are only people, no matter their station in life. As humans, we all stem from the same roots, and we pave our own paths on our journey, whether we turn into teachers, nurses, salespeople, business executives, advertising gurus, engineers, authors, baristas, construction workers, retail managers, lawyers, or even NFL champions.

Each of us is unique, and we all are truly one in a million. Harry taught me to treat people – *all* people – as if this is true.

Chapter Six

Howard, the Nomadic Businessman

Throughout my entire life, I've been told numerous entertaining stories about my parents and their life previous to my existence. Most of the time, these tales and anecdotes are prefaced with, "Things were different back then," and, "You'd never get away with this today," their way of expressing that whatever happened in the story would be completely unacceptable if I were the protagonist instead of them.

My parents are social butterflies, so none of their outlandish stories have ever really shocked me. For as much work as they did throughout their life, they made up for it by socializing in their free time. If there is one thing I've learned from them, it is the key essence of the concept "Work hard, play hard."

Since my parents retired from their careers, it seems as though there has been much more of the playing hard part going on. Recently, they've adhered to that tradition at our weekly Family Dinner Night, where my immediate and extended family gathers for a home-cooked meal. Everyone takes turns hosting the group at their house.

The dinners usually begin with a few appetizers and our favorite alcoholic beverages to accompany the bite-sized food. When the oven dings, indicating that the food is cooked to perfection, we all gather around the dining room table and fill our plates to the brim, then proceed to chow down. As the flowing conversation progresses, somehow we are always reverted back to some of the funniest, most outrageous stories from everyone's past.

The standard venue in which this storytelling takes place is around my parents' dining room table. After a few cocktails, these family parties burst out into story after story, all of us laughing until our sides hurt. Some of the stories are absolutely unforgettable, and this is one of them.

When I unveiled the concept for a conglomerate of stories in this book at one of these family fun-fests, my mother piped up and indicated that she had an adventure to contribute. I had no idea what story she wanted to share as she shuffled into the kitchen to fix herself a dirty martini, complete with bleu cheese-stuffed olives, and waved an arm for me to follow her. She took a sip of her drink and grinned, partly from the sharp bite of the vodka on her tongue, and partly from the nostalgic story she was about to tell me. We plopped down on my parents' large white couch, and my mom began her story.

In 1975, my mother was twenty-four years old. Wise and experienced beyond her years, she ran the Respiratory Therapy Department at one of the local colleges. She was quickly building her career experience and a positive reputation in her field.

Since there were always new products, services, and educational materials emerging in the medical field, she spent a large sum of her time traveling to various conferences around the United States. Every few months, she trekked to a new host city and engaged with the therapists, doctors, nurses, and other medical professionals in the pulmonary field.

Once such adventure was a trip to Miami. She booked her ticket to fly in on Friday night and return early the following Tuesday. Once everything was packed, paid, and ready for the trip, she embarked on the adventure and headed to the airport. She settled into a window seat and waited for her fellow passengers to board the plane. While she waited, she organized her belongings and began collecting her thoughts for the upcoming conference.

A moment later, a man dressed in a suit sat down in the aisle seat of her row and threw her a noncommittal smile. She smirked back and returned to what she was doing. She wanted to focus on the upcoming week of work ahead of her. The flight attendants prepared the aircraft to depart, and the plane was airborne within thirty minutes.

As soon as the plane leveled off at its cruising altitude, the man began a conversation with my mother. She said they instantly clicked and began chatting about their individual lives and the common interests they shared. My mother said she quickly felt very comfortable chatting with Howard.

He introduced himself as "Howard," a businessman who traveled quite a bit for his position. During the week, Howard lived and worked in Chicago. His temporary residence was always The Palmer House Hilton Hotel,* which oozed luxury and expensive adornments and amenities.

Howard was married to a woman who made her permanent home in Miami, so he traveled back and forth every week in order to spend the weekends with her. He was in his mid-fifties and dressed impeccably, every linen noticeably pressed. Since he traveled the same route every week, he was quite familiar with it.

The flight attendants made their way around with the

---

* "The Palmer House" (or so it is called) is still extravagant in 2012. The lobby is immaculate, with elongating drapes, expensive marble, and an impressive front lobby. The hotel hosts professional baseball conferences and many other events. The rooms are modern, dressed with chic tiles and trendy bed linens and window coverings. The charm of this hotel seeps from every angle. The more I learned about Howard, the more I realized he was a man of eclectic and impeccable taste. When my mother mentioned that The Palmer was his home away from home, I was not surprised.

choices of dinner entrees.* Howard and my mother were served drinks with their meal and began consuming the food while continuing their conversation.

All of a sudden, the plane hit what my mother described as "horrible turbulence" and began rocking back and forth. As the bumps perpetuated, passengers began spilling their food all over the seats and tray tables. Drinks went flying into the air and splashed on people's clothing. My mother described the scene as "culinary mayhem, with an overabundance of food strewn all over the plane."

Being the worrywart she is, she began to panic, grasping the arm rails on the side of the seat. She braced herself in anticipation for more vigorous shaking and realized Howard was laughing at her. He sat in his seat calmly and acted as if the atmosphere around him was not in disarray.

My mother managed to somehow curb the nausea that loomed in her stomach and peered over at Howard. His sense of tranquility in an otherwise chaotic moment soothed her worries about the rattling machine around her. He recognized the fear in her eyes and informed her that the patch of turbulence was normal for the part of the skies they were flying through. Each week, as Howard ventured back and forth, he'd been through the same tumultuous air pockets. My mother told me she felt a real sense of relief because of him, and as they initiated another chat, she almost forgot that the plane was shaking so violently.

Howard and my mother spent the rest of the flight going

---

* To put just the concept behind this flight into perspective, consider the year. Since it was 1975, airlines still served full dinners, with metal forks and knives. The flight was considered to be full service, complete with a few courses and varieties of food. For a similar domestic flight in 2012, many carriers serve à la carte chips, peanuts, snacks, and soft drinks. Many times, passengers are required to pay an additional fee for any food or beverages served to them while flying. In addition, the concept of any form of silverware or utensils is mostly null and void. Post September 11, these items have been designated as possible weapons. The flight experience has changed drastically over the years.

back and forth. When I asked my mom for specific details on what they talked about, she couldn't remember exactly. She did remember, though, that she enjoyed the flight with him.

When they began their descent to land, Howard told my mom, "If my wife's in a good mood, we can save you the fare from the airport to your hotel and provide you with a ride." He instructed my mother to wait for him after she collected her luggage from the carousel. His plan was to pull his car around to the arrival area and reconvene with her there. They said goodbye, and my mom scooted off to retrieve her belongings.

When she arrived at the roundabout, she realized her suitcases had arrived before she did; she noticed a shuttle with the name "Fairmont Hotel" plastered across the side, the place where she'd booked for her stay. She hastily chose to take that form of transportation to her hotel. As the bus left, she saw no trace of Howard or his wife in any of the cars they passed.

My mother grabbed dinner with some of her colleagues that night and returned to her room early to rest before the conference the next day. As she was getting ready to climb into bed, she realized that someone had left a message on the hotel room phone line.** She was surprised to hear Howard's voice on the machine. He'd called to tell her that he and his wife had looked for her in the agreed-upon meeting place, but he figured she must have already left. Howard then invited her to join them for a night out on his boat the following evening.

Mom took the opportunity to call him back to accept his invitation. She also asked if she could bring a friend who was attending the conference as well. Howard welcomed my mother and her friend and confirmed a time for the following day.

The next day, she attended the conference and grew increasingly excited about her evening event as the hour approached. She scurried out of the meeting and headed back

---

**   It is important to remember that cell phones were nonexistent in this period of history. As she was telling me the story, I actually asked her why he didn't just call her cell. She rolled her eyes and laughed at me before I could put two and two together.

to her room to take a shower and ready herself, then met her friend Joy in the lobby. Joy asked quite a few questions about my mother's invitation, which seemed to come from a complete stranger. Mom merely brushed off most of the interrogation and chose vague answers for the questions she did choose to answer. In her opinion, Joy was guilty of judging Howard without really knowing who he was, and she refused to give in to the inquiry for that reason.

The two of them loaded up the car and headed to the ocean. When my mother and Joy pulled up to the beachfront, the view was breathtakingly picturesque. Boats sailed in the sunset, and the multicolor horizon was on the brink of sunset. The water glistened in the dimming sunlight as waves rippled onto the beach. A slightly cool breeze grazed the sand.

My mother and Joy made their way through the marina and found the pier that housed Howard's boat. They walked down to the slip he'd told them about and stood there, mesmerized.

My mother prefaced this part of the story with the assumption that she did not know what to expect. She figured Howard's yacht would be elegant and beautiful, but the vessel that floated in front of her was above and beyond her wildest expectations,* seventy-five feet long and utterly spotless. It wasn't just any old boat; it was more like a mini cruise line.

Howard surfaced from the cabin with his wife to greet my mother and her guest. He approached them with a smile and three champagne flutes in hand. In a proud manner, he introduced his gorgeous wife. She shook the hands of my mother and Joy, then smiled, greeting them with welcoming acceptance. The couple accompanied my mom and Joy into the cabin and began the official tour of the boat.

Aside from multiple rooms, bathrooms, and a full lavish

---

* My parents have been boaters for over fifteen years and are quite familiar with the water. They have a very well-kept, solid SeaRay boat of a decent size. For my mother to still be choking on her martini as she described the size of Howard's vessel to me was a prime indicator of just how vast the floating monstrosity was.

galley, it was staffed with a live-in Japanese chef, a housekeeper, and a full-time captain.

Howard made sure the glasses were always topped off, and the four of them chatted over hors d'oeuvres while the main entrées were prepared by the cook. My mother described the evening as something akin to utopian. The four people residing on the boat were in sync with one another, laughing at mutual jokes and reliving personal stories that everyone could relate to with an anecdote of their own. She said it felt like she'd known Howard and his wife for years.

As the night wore on and the hour grew late, Mom and Joy knew they had to get back to their hotel to prepare for the next morning's early meetings. My mother graciously thanked the couple for their hospitality. Howard inquired about them coming back the following night for a sunset ride on the water, and my mother and Joy readily agreed.

This was a pivotal point of the story. Not only did she spend time with a perfect stranger and his wife, but she agreed to return the next night! As I sat on my mother's soft white leather couch, I curled my legs under me to get more comfortable, nestling into the soft confines of the sofa like a little girl in anticipation for the next exciting part of a great fairytale. Everything sounded so magical, and I couldn't wait to hear what happened the second night.

My mom took another sip of her martini; by this point, it was running low, and I wondered if she was going to need a refill. I'm sure my facial expressions gave away my enthusiasm as I smiled and yearned for more.

Unfortunately, instead of a mesmerizing tale of surfing through waves on the vessel, she began the most anticlimactic ending to the story.

It stormed the next evening, with bolts of lightning and clashes of thunder blasting toward Earth. Mother Nature crashed my mother's would-be party, and she had to call Howard to cancel and resume her activities back at the hotel.

Not at all humored by such a cliffhanger, I interrogated

my mother for more information about her adventures: "Did you ever have any contact with Howard after that? When did you see him and his wife again?"

"No…and never."

The phone call was the last verbal communication my mother and Howard would ever have. She shrugged it off as if it was no big deal, adhering to the theory that certain people come into your life for a reason, and that's that.

That most certainly resonated with me. Howard exuded sincerity and generosity. He was one of the most genuine people my mother had ever met, and he enabled her – and vicariously me, through the telling of this story – to witness and experience kindness in an organic way.

Howard knew my mother as a woman he met on an airplane, but treated her and a guest with all the respect he would have given his own family. He was the kind of man who would have given the shirt off of his back just to help someone in need, and when my mother needed support, he was a paternal protector on a rocky airplane ride who put her nerves at ease.

I sat on my mother's couch awestruck in amazement at the tale she shared with me. Howard's willingness to share his life, his home, and his family with my mom and her friend was without restraint. This was not an act of kindness, it was plainly who Howard was at heart. His actions spoke volumes without a single word of his intent. Howard's message was clear.

I asked a few more questions about details next, but my mother was unable to share more with me. She told me that this was the end of the story. I guess I was hoping for some sort of crazy anecdote to continue. At this juncture, it didn't. She reverted back to her maternal instincts.

Of course my mother reiterated again, "Times were different back then, dear, and people have to be much more cautious about their interactions with strangers now." I am not naïve to the violence and danger of the world, but I understood that this was her maternal instinct kicking in. It is her duty as a mother to protect me, even at the ripe old age of twenty-six, similar to the way in which Howard protected her. For as long as I can remember, my mother has tried to protect me from every bad word within an earshot, bloody violence on television, and the classroom bully at my school who threw paper airplanes at me. As you know, the airplane smacked me right in the head, so I didn't avoid all of the world's danger, but I grew as a person because of it. I guess both of us learned a little more from Howard than we realized.

For starters, it's never a bad thing to have people who care about you and can offer you guidance and protection on your journey. There are those you may have known all your life and others you meet along the way, even if only for a few hours on a bumpy airplane ride.

"The world is a different place," she told me, but I disagree with her assumption. The world is the same place it was in 1975. We might have more efficient technology, better access to worldwide communication, and hundreds of thousands of flights that enable us to travel thousands of miles from home within just a few hours, but these are merely adornments. Underneath, we are still all human, and we populate the same big world.

I'm not disagreeing that safety was a looser concept in 1975, but individuals made it that way. There are definite threats to personal safety in a variety of forms today. Howard and my mother taught me that although we need to be cognizant of these dangers, it is equally important to spread genuine kindness, in spite of the vulnerabilities in society. If we could all be so lucky to absorb Howard's lesson, the world would be a better place.

Chapter Seven

Jonah, the Philanthropic Sailor

My sister is a selfless person who regularly volunteers her time to help people in need. She hangs out with a group of friends who call themselves the "Beehive." As long as a free brunch is involved, they are willing to do some backbreaking work to help others out. It is always easier to work for free while goofing around with a group of your ten best friends. The offer of a delicious, all-you-can-eat meal afterward seals the deal.

The Beehive dedicates their spare weekend, holiday, and after-work hours to hang used clothes at a local donation site, pound nails into roofs for Habitat for Humanity, and paint underprivileged schools with a fresh coat of yellow lacquer for a group called Chicago Cares. They are open to nearly any kind of manual labor, as long as they are helping humanity.

Unlike my sister, and embarrassingly enough, I've admittedly never been overly zealous in seeking out opportunities to help others in my spare time. Don't get me wrong: I have a huge heart and am more than willing to help less fortunate people. I just don't actively seek out any kind of work when I have the option to sprawl out on my couch instead.

The classic routine involves my sister sending me a long, drawn-out e-mail about an event she and The Beehive are planning to attend. Knowing me all too well, she lists all the heartwarming and sometimes tear-jerking benefits of the organization in an attempt to tug at my heartstrings, and it normally works. Toward the end of the e-mail, she adds some

My sister (left) and I (right) in about 1987 - best friends from the beginning

sort of sentimental anecdote, beginning with, "Remember how rewarding it was when so and so did such and such..." and incorporates a personally touching tale. Then she indicates the date and time that the volunteer session will occur and begs me to join in the "fun for a few hours" with the promise of the best French toast and fruit salad after the mayhem.

Most of the time, I argue with her at first, providing a few e-mails about the countless other faux obligations I have at that exact same time. But my sister is nothing if not relentless when she is passionate about something, and she just keeps on guilting and tugging. After an average of ten back-and-forth messages, I begrudgingly agree, then sit in front of my computer screen overcome with buyer's remorse. *What did I just agree to?*

By that point, though, it's too late to back out. To my sister, a promise is a promise. Just to confirm, she sends me a Google reminder with a note that goes something like, "Ker, you're really going to enjoy this. I promise." At that point, I'm committed, like it or not, and I can only hope she'll hold up her end of the bargain with fun, enjoyment, and French toast.

I should have known my sister was onto something with all the positive vibes and goodwill she was spreading. Karma has a way of coming back at you like a boomerang. It will either bless you with a smooth landing, right in the palm of your hand, making you proud, or it will hit you upside the head and leave a lump of regret. It can help you in a time of need or serve as

Me standing in front of the Taj Mahal in Agra in 2011

your worst enemy. I'm not necessarily a superstitious person, but I believe what goes around comes around.

Bearing this in mind, I've sleepily surfaced from my bedroom every time I've made a promise to help someone out on my sister's behalf. If nothing else, it is a makeshift insurance plan for my future. If I give back now, *people will do the same when I need their help.*

I never really gave much thought to this until I ventured over to India. Whether it was just a funky coincidence or an actual sign, India is, undeniably, a country that needs help from the other people on the planet. Unfortunately, I was a useless tourist during my brief ten day hiatus to Asia, wandering around aimlessly, drooling over the Taj Mahal, deep crimson-red rock mosques, and some of the worst traffic jams I've ever experienced.

Having grown up amidst Chicago's infamous traffic, I can say that India's traffic jams were unique in both structure and cause. In Chicago, a five-car pile-up can be cleared within a few hours. Accidents are moved to the roadside in a well-choreographed dance of the police, EMT and fire departments, or even to designated accident report sites so that cars can

One of the many cows sitting in the road near Agra, India

continue to snake through the congestion. Cars still retain a position between the two parallel lines that label their lane. Traffic in Chicago – and in the United States in general – is relatively efficiently regulated and almost a pleasure as compared to the rest of the world.

When I was in India, our tour bus got stuck in a traffic

A photo I took in India of cars lined up for miles in 2011

jam for two hours. We were on a five-hour adventure to Agra, home to the beautiful and majestic Taj Mahal. Stopped for such a long time in India's capital city of Delhi, I started to get antsy and asked what was going on. Our tour guide, Sandy, indicated that a cow sitting in the middle of the road. *A cow? Livestock is the cause of this massive confusion of traffic and irritation?* Trust me when I say I almost had a cow at the thought.

My face must have been betrayed my disbelief, because Sandy's next reaction was to explain the religious significance of the animal. In India, cows are sacred. As such, they roam freely, along with snakes, camels, wild dogs, monkeys, elephants, and other creepy crawlers that I spotted at one point or another on the trip. Where's the beef in India? On a pedestal! Cattle are held in high regard that they cannot be forced to move out of the way, even if they are impeding human traffic. In India, I learned the *real* meaning of a traffic jam.

A few days before I experienced the horrific, immovable traffic jam, I found myself on two connecting flights to actually make it out of the homeland and into Asia. The first leg of the flight was a twelve-hour adventure from Chicago's O'Hare International to Istanbul, Turkey. The flight left Chicago at approximately ten thirty p.m. and was scheduled to arrive in Turkey the following day. My plan was to sleep for the duration of the flight so I'd be well rested and ready for the second portion of my journey.

For the most part, I stuck to the plan. Just like any other flight, I called to bid my family and Joe farewell and goodnight and to tell them that I love them. Once I hung up the phone, I knew communication would be relatively sparse for the remainder of my time out of the country, as I didn't want to pay the inflated charges for international airtime while I was away.

The airplane was massive. There were two-seat rows on either side, with an additional dual row in between and another set of five seats across in the middle of the aircraft. The first-class cabin, which I still have never had the luxury of flying in, was to the left as I entered the plane, and my seat was all the way at the back, in the economy section.

I pummeled toward the rear, banging my belongings seat after seat and possibly inadvertently assaulting the poor passengers sitting in the aisle. I reached my seat, tossed my blanket and pillow over to the window, and plopped down in what would be a temporary, upright bed for the next few hours.

I got as comfortable as possible, contorting my body the best I could in such a small space. Seconds later, I noticed a gentleman standing at my row, double-checking his ticket against the aisle numbers posted above the seats. When he verified that he was in the right place, he placed his items in the overhead compartment, sat down next to me, and took a few deep breaths, as if he'd been running a marathon.

The man eventually introduced himself as "Jonah." He was a relatively petite, short man with gray hair and a thick, wispy moustache. His outfit consisted of faded jeans and a blue t-shirt with some sort of emblem on it that I did not recognize. Jonah was soft spoken, his voice almost inaudible and squeaky, requiring me to really tune in to hear what he had to say. We made the initial small talk and introduced ourselves, explaining to one another our motives for being on a flight to Turkey.

I told Jonah all about my upcoming adventures in India, though I really had no idea what I was in for. I also described the in-depth preparation for my trip. My fellow peers and I had traveled around the world, studying to earn our MBAs. We had taken part in multiple video and chat sessions, connecting via Skype to discuss our readings for the week. We had interviewed native Indians from the region where we were headed, and we'd watched *Outsourced*, a film depicting Indian business practices and how the global market was intertwined within them. I thought I knew it all, and I conveyed that to Jonah.

I didn't spend much time talking about my family, friends, or my job, simply because those usual go-to items didn't seem to cross my weary, but goal-driven mind. I could only revel in the fact that I was headed to a country where I'd be unfamiliar with the native language. I was nervous to head across the world by myself, and that became obvious to my fellow traveler as I rambled endlessly about my adventure. Still, the gracious Jonah only smiled and listened to my banter. After about ten or fifteen minutes, I realized that I was more than dominating the conversation. I stopped myself and apologized for my behavior, then politely asked him to tell me about himself.

Jonah began the conversation by telling me that he was headed to Israel to meet up with his wife and two daughters. While he was of Israeli descent, he was an American, and his family had been waiting for him there for the last two months. When I asked how and why he had gone to the United States, he told me he was actually just flying through the U.S. on a trek home from a set of private islands in the Pacific Ocean. Jonah was a world-traveling sailor.

Boating has been near and dear to my heart for a long time. I recall my childhood years aboard my parents' vessel, screaming for them to slow down. According to their version of the story, I ruined every ride we ever took because I didn't want them to speed up to more than five miles per hour.

Though I do not doubt their story, it is difficult for me to imagine not loving the wind blowing in my hair, forging over the boat wake on a pair of skis, or the burning sensation of the water rushing into my nose when I fly off of an inner tube. I must have developed a need for splish-splashing speed somewhere in my lifetime, because as an adult, I literally cannot get enough when it comes to water sports.

My parents used to drag me out onto their boat every weekend. I took up fishing as a hobby to busy myself while they mingled with their equally nautical friends. I begged my dad every week to take me to the bait store and buy worms for me. When we got to the marina, I couldn't bear to actually touch the worms, so Dad baited my hook for me, and off I went. As soon as I pulled up a flopping, slimy creature on the other end of my pole – which I did quite often – I would race back down the pier toward my dad so he could take the fish off the hook for me. Clearly, in fishing, this is the way to go – all of the fun and none of the yuck.

Still, my boating experience was quite limited in comparison to Jonah's. I was confined to the freshwater wonders of Lake Michigan and Lake Shaffer. Our family would take the boat out for the day and float aimlessly around the water, soaking in the sun and the cool breeze and enjoying an occasional, refreshing swim. It was such a leisurely adventure that three-foot waves intimidated me, even though most sailors would pass them off as nothing more than a ripple. My overprotective father would never think about putting our mother or my sister and me in danger, so I really can't recall why I was so terrified.

Jonah, on the other hand, sailed around the world to

remote islands and unique ports. He owned a thirty-seven-footer, a sailboat. The vessel, powered by a small engine and a massive mast, propelled Jonah and his family through the darkest depths of the ocean – and waves much larger than the three-foot ones that petrified me.

My eyes lit up. I was intrigued by his bravery, traveling by water almost everywhere he went. A thousand questions must have circulated through my head as I pondered the sea-faring family, and I asked him as many as I could. The first one was, "What are the largest waves you've ever been caught in?"

Jonah looked over at me and smiled a genuine-looking grin, then took another deep breath before his answer came out. "Well, we were caught in a severe storm once. Yielded thirty-five-foot waves!"

My mouth dropped open at the thought, as something like that would have likely given me a heart attack. I couldn't even fathom how large that really was.*

He laughed a little in understanding; his seasoned family was even frightened by that storm. After they took cover and the storm had a chance to simmer down, they reconvened on the deck to put the boat back together. Ropes were frayed at the ends, buoys were flipped over, and all of the decorations on the outside of the watercraft had been fed to the hungry ocean monster as a sacrifice. He and his family were thankful they'd all survived.

As he was talking, I started putting two and two together about his situation, and that prompted my second question. Since Jonah was sitting next to me on the airplane, heading to Istanbul, and his family was temporarily visiting Israel, I had to wonder where his boat was. When I asked, he chuckled a little to himself and reported that it was off the coast of Thailand, in the Pacific Ocean. He then whipped out his phone and showed me

---

* To get a grip on the size of this wave, I went to Google and searched for the popular show, The Deadliest Catch. In an episode covering a ridiculous amount of storms, I learned just how monstrous the storm was. If you want to see for yourself, there is a clip on YouTube at http://www.youtube.com/watch?v=sor5KTqNdxk.

the most picturesque view of a body of water I'd ever seen, like something right off of a postcard.*

The photo was an aerial shot of the surrounding land and water where his boat was docked. There were rugged mountains guarding a fleet of stark white boats floating in a body of deep turquoise waters. Multicolored flowers, brush, bushes, and trees adorned the mountains. The landscape looked like something right off the pages of a home gardening magazine, but it was on a much larger scale than any one person could ever achieve. It was, for lack of a better word, perfect.

Jonah pointed to a miniscule dot of a boat on the picture and said, "There she is," beaming like a proud papa. Clearly, the boat was his baby.

I stared at the phone in awe of what my eyes were registering. He read my reaction and could tell I was utterly impressed. The more intrigued I became, the more I wanted to chat with him. This sparked my third question: "Why do you spend your time traveling around the world on your boat?"

He paused for a moment to think about his answer. I could tell there was quite a long explanation for it, and I was ready to hear it; after all, I had the next eleven and a half hours to do nothing but sit there and listen. I could sleep anytime. It wasn't every day I could interview a modern-day Robinson Crusoe.

He began by informing me that he had always thought of himself as a philanthropist. By definition, that is a person who performs charitable or benevolent actions, exhibiting a love for humankind; in other words, a person who donates his or her time simply to help others. I immediately thought of my sister.

Unlike most humanitarians, spreading goodwill toward men was not only Jonah's passion, but also his livelihood. He literally thrived off of the satisfaction he got from helping others. Jonah and his wife had children at a young age and embraced

---

*   Of course I've seen beautiful photographs in brochures, advertisements, movies, video clips, and other forms of commercial media, but the amazing thing about this one was that it was a snapshot taken on his personal cell phone.

the chance to travel around the world as a family. Jonah had always loved to sail and decided it would be the best form of transportation to live his dream of experiencing global culture and to share it with his family.

So he and his wife homeschooled their children from the confines of their boat and traveled from port to port. When they reached a new area, Jonah and his family volunteered their time to help people. It didn't matter what they decided to do, as long as they were doing something to better the lives of those they met.

I asked Jonah to tell me the most rewarding experience he'd had with his family on their journeys. Secretly, it was a selfish request. I hoped his devotion might somehow rub off on me. As I mentioned, anytime my sister begged me to donate my time, I griped about the request, pretty much until my work was complete. I was hoping Jonah would inspire some sort of epiphany that would change my views on volunteering. I *wanted to want* to help others.

Jonah took another deep breath before beginning his story. He asked if I was familiar with the destruction that had occurred as a result of Hurricane Katrina. I nodded to indicate I'd heard of it, and he went on to explain.

Jonah and his family were inland in the U.S. when that devastating hurricane struck the southern part of the country near New Orleans. Although they did not know the initial brutality of the storm, they noticed the intensity in the eyes and voices of the shocked reporters on the news. The story unfolded through the media, and the severity of the devastation grew more intense. He said that as he watched the brutal images of desperation from his fellow Americans, he couldn't help but feel the need to help somehow, even if only by donating his time and energy.

Many of the relief volunteers were told to stay out of the region to reduce the danger of congestion while authorities worked day in and day out to clean up the mess. Jonah and his family patiently waited until they were able to take the initiative to help.

Weeks and months passed after the storm, and Jonah continued to think about the unfortunate souls who'd been rendered homeless, living in shelters without their personal belongings, their memories smashed into a watery oblivion. So many had lost everything, and a whole town was in ruins. For him, this hit home. He described the feeling as "gut-wrenching" and couldn't hardly bear to think about the misery the storm had caused for so many. *What if it had been my family?* Jonah wondered. He said it reminded him of the massive storm he'd encountered on his boat, and that made him thankful that they'd only experienced such insignificant damage by comparison. Jonah took that as his cue, and he decided it was his time to help.

Jonah and his family temporary lived in the New Orleans vicinity for four weeks. Each day, they devoted countless hours to cleaning up the debris that was strewn all over the landscape. They worked alongside families, friends, and perfect strangers, cohesive groups of people trying to help in the wake of a horrible disaster. Everyone listened to one another and worked together. The efforts were not flawless, but everyone had a collective goal: to put the city back together, give to the people in need, and find solutions to the problems Katrina had caused.

Jonah described the experience as beyond rewarding. He met hundreds of volunteers while collectively rebuilding the lives of many others. The families, children, and locals were so grateful for the donation of time, money, manpower, and resources. They were overcome with emotion by the altruistic nature of the people who helped. I was impressed by Jonah's story. The effort wasn't about him or his family getting the glory or the thanks. It was all about the people in need, the people they were all working so hard to help. Jonah and his family were leaders.

They set idealistic examples for all people to contribute back to the community. Unfortunately, much of the time, energy, and resources that Jonah's family and others like him had to offer went unnoticed. Still, he didn't do it to be recognized as some kind of martyr, but offering a helping hand, a gesture of kindness from the bottom of his heart. He *wanted* to be there, and he didn't desire any recognition for it.

I thought about Jonah for a long time after we parted ways when the flight ended. I ended up drifting off into a deep

Volunteering at Miriam's Kitchen in Washington D.C. on a personal trip there preparing and serving breakfast to homeless people.

sleep after our brief conversation. His impact lasted much longer than the sixty minutes of conversation we shared, and his story brought back a personal memory from a year prior to that moment.

Back in 2010, eleven months before I met Jonah, I took a trip to New Orleans with The Beehive in search of some Southern hospitality, Cajun-style cuisine, and live jazz music at a huge festival hosted by New Orleans each year. My sister propositioned me about the trip and promised that we would also be going to Bourbon Street. As an avid and very passionate traveler, I wanted to experience the culture and city; thus, I accepted the invitation almost immediately.

After I booked my flight on A+ Airlines to travel there, I received a copy of the itinerary via e-mail. We would spend a total of four days exploring the ins and outs of the French-inspired region. The first day, we would go skeet-shooting and indulge in homemade barbequed shrimp,* accompanied by ice-cold beer.

A Jazz Fest** was scheduled for two of the other days. The final activity just said "Habitat for Humanity," so I put a phone call into my sister to ask about this. She started her normal spiel about volunteering, promising that I'd really enjoy myself, which I doubted. I did not have much of a choice in the matter, so I listened and retained an indifferent attitude about it.

Our volunteering day came too quickly for my taste, on the third day of our trip. We woke up early and put on "work clothes," as I like to call them, ready to head out to help build houses in the Ninth Ward. One of the poorest parishes in New Orleans, it did not receive the financial resources or physical labor it needed post-Katrina, so Habitat for Humanity had stepped in to try and rebuild some of the demolished homes for the dislocated people there. They designed them to fit the needs of the families who would call them home.

---

* Traditional barbequed shrimp was one of the most delectable treats of food that I ate on my trip. It was homemade by a friend's mother, flavored with locally grown spices and a rich, aromatic broth. We dipped chunks of French bread in the aftermath of the juice to soak up the remaining morsels of zest. The amount of shrimp our group consumed was gluttonous.

** Jazz Fest is an annual two-week tradition to celebrate the Southern style of jazz at the beginning of May. Artists from all over the world gather to play for massive audiences. The festival is hosted on the fairgrounds, in a laidback atmosphere. Vendors serve crawfish etouffee, homemade seafood jambalaya, shrimp po'boy, and scrumptious, warm peach cobbler with a dollop of vanilla ice cream floating on the top. Not only are visitors surrounded by musical prodigies, but they also get an authentic taste of classic New Orleans cuisine.

It was seven a.m. when we arrived at our construction site, and I was less than enthused to be working on vacation. Two Habitat for Humanity representatives were there to instruct our group on what to do. I was assigned to Group Two, which was heading to another site to work on a different house. I followed my peers and tried to wake myself up out of my drowsy mindset.

We approached our worksite, and our leader showed us a box filled with tools. He pointed us in the direction of the ladder and motioned for us to bring it over to the back of the house. We had roof duty, and the edges of the roof were the next step in the process that needed to be completed. He asked if any of us were scared of heights, and the majority of my teammates shrieked at the mention of altitude changes. Having gone skydiving four times, I could not honestly report that I suffered from acrophobia, so I stepped up and volunteered to pound nails into the roof some twenty feet in the air.

Although the work was grueling, the profuse beads of sweat dripping down my face were satisfying. I kept pounding harder and harder, eventually swinging into a groove. Don't get me wrong: I did not enjoy the brutal physical labor by any means.

When the instructor indicated it was lunchtime, I jumped at the opportunity for a break and was the first one to step up and order my meal. I failed to savor any of the food, though, and considered it simply an energy source instead of a sensory enjoyment for my taste buds. When I finished, I craved more calories to replace all the ones I'd spent up on the rooftop, but it was time for us to head back and finish our assignment.

The assignment for the second half of our day was to prep the window wells for installation. As instructed, we filled the empty openings with some sort of liner that would keep drafts out of the house. To me, this contribution seemed almost insignificant, but our team finished every window by the time we were supposed to leave the site. By then, I was physically exhausted.

The entire process lasted for a whole day, and the

instructor thanked us for our services to the organization. We cleaned up the small mess we'd made and collected our belongings. I hopped in the conversion van to head back to the condo where we were lodging, eager to shower and sit down for a nice dinner.

Until I met Jonah, I had never really taken the opportunity to reflect back on those services. The house we'd worked on didn't seem like much more than an empty building – a dull, vacant structure. I had helped install the roof and prep the windows, but that mere eight hours of work seemed so insignificant in the grand scheme of things. We only accomplished two tasks, and when we left, there was still so much to be done to that house and so many other houses and lives that were in dire need of being rebuilt. There was no emotional attachment to the house for me; it was nothing but a conglomeration of wood pieces conjoined to create a larger structure. Jonah's story changed my perspective quite a bit. It wasn't about the edifice we were building. It was about the family we were building it for.

My chat with Jonah forced me to consider the end result. We were creating a dwelling that a family could thrive in. Instead of living in shelters created for the victims of Katrina, they would become proud owners of a property where their children could grow up happy, healthy, safe, and provided for. This had nothing to do with the house, volunteering, or New Orleans. It had far more to do with humanity than with habitat, and through Jonah's anecdote, I was able to see it as more than just a day's work. We spent eight hours there, and the payoff for our good deeds would be years for a family to thrive, grow, and share a life within the confines of those walls. They would, quite literally, have a roof over their heads because of our efforts, and that made me feel good deep down inside.

My work on the roof and windows was only a tiny piece of the puzzle, but it didn't seem so insignificant after I spoke with Jonah, a true philanthropist. My contribution, along with the ready, willing, and able people who volunteered before and after me, allowed a home to be built. In reality, we accomplished much more than two tasks, because what we really built for that family was the foundation for a new life. At the time of my service, there didn't seem to be any emotions tied to it, but those precious memories and feelings would develop as the house became a home, and that would only come with time.

Jonah never knew how much he helped me, as I, myself, did not realize the impact of his words until I took the time to reflect on them long after we'd gone our separate ways. On the airplane, I was too hyped up about flying across the world to truly digest what he was saying to me, and I didn't take the time to do so until a few weeks later.

I wish I could go back and thank Jonah for the perspective he provided. I can't claim that he was all the motivation I needed to suddenly morph into some sort of philanthropic guru who volunteers every weekend; however, I *would* venture to say that I think about helping others much more now. I now realize the impact I can have over another person's life is endless. It just takes a time and perseverance.

I don't worry about volunteering in the future. There will be ample opportunities, at the very least, in the form of e-mails from my sister, and I will have plenty of chances to lend a helping hand here and there. I have no doubt that she will continue to use her persuasiveness on me, and most of the time, I'll agree, albeit after an argument or two. She knows just how to push the right buttons. We will continue to argue back and forth until I reluctantly give in to her request. And of course, if all else fails, she knows I can never turn down a decent brunch.

In my future acts of service to others, I will reflect on what I learned from Jonah. I can't help but think of his perspective on the process of giving back. Who knows? Maybe Jonah and I will meet again on one of these ventures.

Chapter Eight

Kenny, the Floating Jeweler

When I was a kid, the image of someone soaring through the sky beneath a parachute mesmerized me, and I've been enamored with it ever since. I have always admired the kind of bravery it would take to plummet to the Earth, at the mercy of the wind, gravity, and a thin piece of fabric. I would stare at their cheeks flapping in the wind while they gasped for air and giggled simultaneously. The best part about it was that no one really had the same reaction to the jump, the free fall, or the landing; it seems to be a brand new experience each and every time.

It appeared that the parachute manufacturers always chose the most vibrant colors to sew together to form the awning. Bright amethyst purples, deep midnight blues, and canary yellow mixes were my absolute favorite. Every chute seemed to have its own unique pattern, characterizing the jumper who relied on the umbrella to carry them down.

A few times as a kid, I saw people plummeting toward the Earth into a grassy field as my parents drove during family vacations down a major highway. I would stare up at the clouds, piecing them together and thinking about how vast the world really was. Once the glimpse of a tie-dyed floating object caught my eye, I lost myself in my own imagination.

I wondered what the people were thinking about and what the world must have looked like from their vantage point so high above the clouds. Sure, I had flown in an airplane, but the thick glass of those windows is more intended for safety than an invite to view the surface below. The openness of the parachute allows a skydiver to gain an organic sense of Earth, or so I thought.

I was jealous of the person flying toward the ground. I wanted that experience of flying with fabric wings. I might have only been twelve or thirteen years old, but I made a conscious promise to myself that it was something I would make sure to do in the future.

I planned to skydive as soon as my legal age would permit me to do so. I chose not to share my plan with my parents, as I did not want to be dissuaded by their negative reaction. Even at the age of twelve, I knew both of them would look at me with a roll of the eyes and a shake of the head. If they had anything to say about it, I would never skydive. Like any normal parents, they were protective, and few moms and dads would want their little girl jumping out of an airplane.

Lucky for me, I am an economist. One of the most intrinsic characteristics of such a career is that we believe in data and statistics. Many of the theories and assumptions we follow are built upon the numerical facts that statistics unveil. When I hit the age threshold to legally be eligible to jump out of the airplane,* I took it upon myself to learn a little bit more about it before my first attempt. I decided to base my judgment of the sport's safety on the number of injuries and fatalities incurred in the past. Economics had always served me well, so it seemed logical for me to apply the theories in every facet of my life.

---

* Most skydiving schools require individuals to be at least eighteen years of age for legal and liability reasons. The ones I attended would not even allow an underage individual jump without parental consent.

According to the United States Parachute Association (USPA), there were only twenty-one related fatalities in 2010. This may seem like a lot, but the number of total jumps recorded by the association was three million. This means there were 0.007 fatalities per 1,000 jumps.

In other words, the likelihood of dying from a parachute jump is minute. The statistics reported for the last twelve years have been similar, indicating that the consistency in safety has been upheld. The association also reported that number of fatalities have remained under fifty since 1998.

In order to put this into perspective, I looked up the death toll for motor vehicle accidents during the same timeframe. People use cars every day to get to their destinations on the surface instead of from above the surface. In 2009, the United States Center for Disease Control (CDC) reported that 33,808 individuals died in motor vehicle accidents. Although there are far more car rides in any given year than individual skydives, the overwhelming death toll is far higher and statistically relevant. To me, this information was like a flashing green light, telling me that jumping out of an airplane was something I simply had to experience.

By the time I made the decision, I was on the cusp of graduating with two undergraduate degrees from Indiana University. When the big day finally came for me to close the books for the last time, my family overwhelmed me with a splash of celebratory mayhem in Bloomington, Indiana.

Both of my parents, my best friend, and my sister drove down to shower me with congratulations the entire weekend. They all attended my grueling two-hour ceremony in the field house, where the temperature continually rose to a stifling eighty-two degrees. We took tons of pictures after the ceremony and relished over dinner about how proud they were of me. I felt like a million bucks.

Later that night, we ventured over to Kirkwood, one of the most popular streets in Bloomington. It is lined with college bars that serve delicious, inexpensive drinks, play live music, and guarantee a great time. After a few rounds of drinks, the idea of skydiving came to me. I could think of no better way to celebrate my college graduation than stepping out of an airplane from thousands of feet in the air. As illogical as it might seem, I couldn't think of anything more logical at the time.

Overjoyed with excitement and enthusiasm, which is the norm under most circumstances for me, I ran over to my sister in the bar and told her about the plan. From the beginning, she had a beaming smirk across her face. When I finished, she took a large gulp of her drink and insisted that she would join me.

We were going to make the jump together, and it would be a unique experience for both of us. I was on top of the world! I had received my diploma and graduated to alumni status, lined up a promising job to start the following month, and would check a major milestone off of my bucket list the following week – likely long before I got anywhere near kicking the bucket. I was elated and was ready to conquer the clouds.

Our parents did not share the same enthusiasm when we dropped the bomb about our skydiving plans for the following weekend. Not only would *one* of their children be risking her life, but now both of their daughters would be hurling toward the planet beneath a parachute. My mom told us that it sickened her to think about it. She did not want to hear any details until after we were done.

My dad, on the other hand, went into denial about it. I don't think he actually believed that either one of us would ultimately have the guts to make good on our crazy threat. For his sake, we limited our discussion about it, knowing he's always been a worry-wart.

It was Saturday, May 10, 2008 when my sister and I would take our leap, and it seemed surreal that the day had finally arrived. After waiting more than twenty-one years for that fateful day, envying those skydivers on television and beyond the highway skies, I was more than anxious. My sister picked me up early in the morning to drive out to the venue where we'd made our reservations.

We arrived on time and strolled into the hangar to sign the paperwork. Until that point in my life, I had never made any extensive purchases such as a house, so I had no concept of "signing my life away." The customer service agent behind the counter handed me a stack of papers thicker than some of my textbooks.

She instructed both of us to initial every short blank line in the text; I didn't count the actual number of slots, but I would guess there were at least seventy-five. We were to sign and date the final piece of paper, and we had to provide a copy of our state-issued identification card. My sister and I gave one another a look and returned to our seats to begin our assignment. This was going to be fun!

When my sister and I read those documents, we had to chuckle a bit. In a lot of legalese and disclaimer jargon, the verbiage strongly stated that if we were injured or died during the jump, the company would assume no responsibility. That was what we were signing ourselves up for. I suppose it's best to elaborate on these declarations that we initialed verbatim, complete with bolding and capitalization:

I UNDERSTAND THAT MY VOLUNTARY PARTICIPATION and/or ASSOCIATION IN THE COVERED ACTIVITIES WILL EXPOSE ME TO THE UNAVOIDABLE RISK OF MAJOR OR PERMANENT INJURY, PAIN, SUFFERING, AND/OR DEATH.

I HAVE CAREFULLY READ THIS CONTRACT AND UNDERSTAND ITS CONTENTS. I AM SIGNING THIS CONTRACT AGREEMENT OF MY OWN FREE WILL, WITHOUT DURESS. **It has been explained to me, and I understand that by signing this Legal Contract, I am giving up important legal rights. It is my intent to do so.**

These were pretty intimidating sentences to sign off on before engaging in a sport. To be honest, I didn't read through all of the hairy details of jumbled words. Some of the phrases stuck out more than others, but I knew what we were getting ourselves into by jumping out of an aircraft hovering in the air, and I was still ready to skydive. In my envy, of all the other jumpers I had already signed up for it a decade ago, long before I slapped my initials on all those forms.

We completed the weighty task at hand and asked for directions to our instructors. The employee pointed to a series of monitors mounted in a few corners of the building and told us we'd be good to go when our names appeared in the lineup. "When you see your name," she said, "you can head to flight school to be trained and prepped for your dive."

We welcomed the time to watch other divers make their first jumps through the sky. The airplane would take off, and within ten minutes, we would see small spots of color floating in the air. The figures gradually grew larger and more recognizable as the person plunged toward Earth.

After another ten minutes, the people landed safely in the grassy knoll. They picked up the chutes and brought them back into the hangar to be repacked. Their reactions were as diverse as they were hilarious. Some were extremely overwhelmed, and others laughed with joy. Needless to say, we thoroughly enjoyed people-watching that day.

After a few hours, both of us agreed to head to the snack shop to grab a bite to eat before our big adventure. At that point in my life, I was unsure about the sustainability of my stomach at 120 miles per hour, the rate at which gravity pulls a skydiver to Earth when they jump out of an airplane in free fall. I purchased a few light snacks to tide me over. As we nibbled, both of us complained about the waiting time. It was far past our original reservation timeslot, and we were well beyond ready to jump.

More than an hour after our miniscule lunch, our names were finally posted on the screen. We walked over to the school for training and to prep for our plunge. Since we were going to be on the same flight, we met up with our individual instructors.

They told both of us to pick out a jumpsuit and to put it on over our clothing. I walked over to a long bar of hangers filled with jumpsuits that had been worn over and over again by past jumpers. I chose the most vibrant, highlighter-green uniform. I had to almost yank it on because it was a tight fit over my clothing. My sister wore a bright red suit, so the two of us made quite a Christmas-looking pair.

After we were dressed and ready for takeoff, my sister and I spent a few minutes taking pictures of each other and of us together. We wanted the memories of our skydive to last forever. The attire that adorned our bodies was tangible proof that it was actually going to take place. We wore massive grins on our faces as we snapped those Kodak moments, forever capturing our brave feat on film.

Our instructors quickly summoned us back over to the hangar, as we would be part of the next cohort to make a dive. Paul, our instructor, held up my safety harness for me to step into the leg holes, and after I did so, he pulled them up. He put the shoulder straps over my arms and began adjusting and tightening each of the four pliable points on the unit.

When I felt like I couldn't move any of my limbs, he handed me a lilac-purple altimeter that strapped to my fingers to indicate the elevation level; I would use that device to know the exact moment to pull my parachute open. He also found a pair of plastic and elastic safety glasses for my eyes. When I tried the goggles on, they smashed my nose down and put a dent in the skin on my face, but they had to remain extra tight so they would not fly off during free fall.

With all of my equipment in place, it was finally time for us to discuss the procedure and safety tips for the jump. He pointed to four metal clamps that would connect me to his parachute, since he would be jumping in tandem with me. On our flight up to 14,000 feet, the altitude scheduled for our initial jump, Paul would lock the clamps together to ensure they were secure. I was to put on my safety glasses and check my altimeter while he did so.

Once we were out of the airplane, Paul and I would free fall for a total of sixty seconds. At 6,500 feet above ground, I was to indicate with hand gestures when I was going to pull the ripcord to open the parachute that would glide us to a safe landing. Paul informed me that during this time, it was critical to remember to get the parachute open in enough time to float to the ground safely; that was one of the main reasons why master and student would be connected. If I forgot on my first jump, he would be there to pull the cord for me. In essence, and in spite of all those disclaimers, the process was virtually foolproof.

While I was learning the ropes of jumping out of an aircraft, a quirky man with a charismatic attitude walked over to introduce himself. He shook my hand and told me his name was "Kenny," a videographer who would the once-in-a-lifetime experience for us. His outgoing personality was uplifting, and his physical appearance mirrored it.

He was wearing helmet on his head, with a camera affixed to the top, and he held an additional camcorder in his hands. He looked ridiculous, but he couldn't have cared less. His main concern was to capture a memory for me. He gave me a few high-fives and began the filming process, capturing my training session, nervous jitters, and enthusiastic excitement. I knew Kenny would make my experience unforgettable, but what would actually happen was far beyond my expectations.

Almost immediately after going through three rounds of practice stretches, moving my arms in the correct patterns, the airplane pulled up in front of the hangar. The loud buzzing of the whipping propellers was almost deafening, and I couldn't even hear Paul's instructions from five feet away. He pointed over to the airplane, and I started walking.

Kenny was goofing around with his camera, asking me questions about the jump that I really didn't know the answers to, just to get me smiling for the camera. To be honest, most of the captured imagery on the DVD I purchased from my first skydive included intricate details that I initially missed. In the moment, I was enraptured in the sounds, smells, sights, and sensory overload that my body was experiencing. Lucky for me, it was not Kenny's first time to film a first-timer; he was a true professional who knew all the perfect sentiments to capture to tell the whole story.

As we approached the plane, I realized that my sister was

Getting ready to jump out of the airplane with all of my gear on

far behind me in the line of people who were boarding. It was too late for me to turn back. Paul could see that I was worried about her, and he reassured me that she was in good hands, even though she ended up being the very last diver to enter the plane.

I didn't quite know what to expect when I entered the plane. The cordial etiquette that is typically the job of flight attendants was irrelevant. Since it was such a small flier, we entered through a door in the back of the plane. There were no seats, aisles, or even seatbelts. It was furnished by only one large cushion stretched from the front of the craft near the pilots to the back door.

I crawled on my knees to the front of the airplane, and Paul told me to sit, cross-legged, directly in front of him. He rested his back on the metal separator that divided the pilots from the passengers. Kenny parked himself straight ahead of me so he could capture the pre-jump preparations on tape.*

I saw my sister look back with a smile on her face; clearly, she was as excited as I was. Before I knew it, the engines were roaring at full throttle, and we were speeding down the runway. There was no turning back. My only escape route was to hurl myself out the back door at 14,000 feet in the air.

I was at the mercy of a piece of fabric and my instructor, whom I'd known for a whopping twenty minutes. My adrenaline was pumping through my veins on overdrive, and I was overcome with a flood of emotions: anxiety, exhilaration, anticipation, and liberation.

It turned out to be the shortest flight I'd ever been on.** From the time we took off, I was given last-minute instructions and tips, to which I listened attentively. I was able to justify the risk I was about to take that way, as the more knowledge I had, the less dangerous it seemed. Paul went over the most important part a few more times: "Cross your arms when you are going to release the parachute at 6,500 feet." This was the single most valuable piece of information I had received that day.

---

* While writing this, I was inspired to dig my skydiving DVD out from the archives. I watched it a few times over and over again and reminisced in the glory of the experience. Many of the minute details are very vivid in the video, and it is still an absolute treat to watch some four years later, thanks to Kenny's amazing eyes and ears and his propensity for knowing which of those moments I would hold most dear.

** The second-shortest flight I've taken was from Chicago, Illinois to Grand Rapids, Michigan. This flight pattern is approximately eighteen minutes, a puddle-jump over Lake Michigan. Strangely enough, the flight to India that I took was equal in price to this route.

Jumpers began piling out one after another in synchronized time intervals. That part of the trip seemed to be somewhat of a blur. There were so many things to remember that I did not have time to fathom the fact that my sister was out of the plane and had already jumped. As I tried to recall all that I needed to know, my sibling's body was plummeting toward the Earth, and I hoped she was enjoying her trip. My turn was coming right up.

I followed the directions to prepare myself with all of the safety equipment provided to me. I checked my altimeter to ensure that it was registering the correct reading of elevation. Once all safety checks and preparations were complete, Paul, Kenny, and I began wiggling on our knees toward the door.

I grabbed the safety glasses that were hanging off of my neck and pulled them up over my eyes; as I did so, the elastic strap clipped my pearl earrings and ripped one of the studs out of my ear. I panicked, for it was the worst possible time to lose such a sentimental piece of jewelry. I was supposed to be queuing up to make my jump.

Kenny must have seen the panic in my face and asked what was wrong. We were the only three people left in the rear of the aircraft, but when I told him that I'd lost my earring, the three of us milled around briefly to look for it. I didn't see it anywhere. I kept turning from side to side, desperate to find my jewelry, but the harness restricted my movement. I had to find that earring.

Time was working against us, because at that very moment, the pilots were giving us clearance to jump. I gave up hope of finding it. Although I was disappointed, I knew could always buy a new pair of pearl earrings. A first skydive, on the other hand, was a once-in-a-lifetime opportunity for me.

As Paul and I approached the door, Kenny perched himself outside the airplane, clinging to the railing as if he were made of Velcro. We scooted over to the opening and sat there for what seemed like forever. I overlooked squared grids of rural land, unable to make out anything with much clarity from that elevation. I had anticipated I would feel a burst of panic in that moment, but I didn't. Rather, I was simply mesmerized by the bird's-eye view of the world.

Within a few seconds, Paul pushed us both out of the plane, and a feeling of weightlessness overcame my body. We

My sister and I seconds after we landed our first skydive in 2008

completed a back-flip* in the air out of the plane and leveled off in a belly-flop position shortly thereafter. I regained my balance and consciousness and realized I was floating through the clouds.

Many people have asked me if the initial free fall feels like the stomach drop people get on a rollercoaster hill, but I'd have to say no. I don't know the intricate physics behind the momentum and pull of gravity, but I know how I felt. I was floating at 120 miles per hour with a ton of wind smacking me in the face, and

---

* This was the first time I'd ever completed an actual back-flip in my life, and being suspended in the air made it seem simple. The fact that I really had no control over my body position was an even larger factor. This is a noteworthy event in my life because of my devotion as a child to gymnastics. For all those years while my mother paid for me to attend lessons, I was never able to do a back-flip. Finally, it was mission accomplished, courtesy of weightlessness on my very first skydive.

the feeling was surreal.

Kenny, my ever-capable videographer, somehow steered himself over to where Paul and I were. In a playful manner, he grabbed my hand to spin me around and around above the Earth. Since it was my first time jumping out of an airplane, I was preoccupied with the technical details, particularly measuring my altitude to make sure I pulled the parachute on time. Kenny was pointing at something in his hand, but I couldn't make out what it was, and I assumed he was instructing me to look at my altimeter. When I looked, I determined that we were at 7,000 feet above the Earth and still falling freely.

During our final descent in free fall, my eyes were glued to my device, waiting to know when I should pull the parachute that would, in essence, save us from being turned into pancakes.

My first solo sky dive floating about one hundred feet above ground

As we neared the 6,500 mark, I crossed my arms to signal that I was about to pull the reins. A split second later, I grabbed the red rubber ball that was connected to the outside of the pack to let the parachute rip into the air. It deployed and inflated, and I instantly felt my legs swinging up into a pike position. Our speed slowed within milliseconds to a swift twenty-five miles per hour for the remaining ten-minute glide to the ground.

Kenny had separated from us for safety to prevent the parachutes from getting twisted up in one another. He sped up his flight to the ground by controlling the reins to the chute. He focused on grounding himself to capture the landing of my dive on video. The remainder of my first skydive was a lesson.

Paul took the time to show me how to steer the device. We made turns to both sides, altering the turn radius for each. He talked me through the procedure of landing the balloon safely on the ground. As he steered us to our destination, I was to lift my legs in a pike position to prepare to land on my butt – the most efficient way for a first-timer to avoid injury. I hung underneath the canopy in awe of the beautiful world I live in. It was an experience I would never forget, and as I listened to Paul's instructions, I was almost in a dazed state, soaking in my unforgettable surroundings.

My time under the parachute was limited to a mere ten minutes. I actually asked Paul if there was a way to prolong the glide in that utopian atmosphere, but I didn't get the answer I was hoping for. It was time for us to land, and I did not want the experience to be over.

When we landed, Kenny was already waiting for us on the ground, with his camera rolling. I helped to steer the lines down to the ground and lifted my legs up when we were close enough to the surface. When we actually touched down, I had a hard time remaining on my feet, and it took a few tries before I was able to stand up on my own. While Kenny interviewed me for feedback on the experience, I was overwhelmed with emotion. It was one of the most energizing things I'd ever participated in, and when he asked what my favorite part of the dive was, I replied that it was the initial fall out of the plane.

I saw my sister stumbling over from a few feet away, and I ran up to give her a hug. I could not wait to hear her reaction to the jump, but something wasn't right; her face was ghost white, and I had never seen her so pale. A feeling of worry overtook my body. When I asked if she was okay, she replied that she just didn't feel good. She wanted something to eat and drink to regain her strength from the jump, and she'd gotten quite disoriented and dizzy on the way back to Earth. I put my arm around her to escort her back to the snack shop for a granola bar and a can of pop.

Just as we were about to leave, Kenny appeared before us in the grassy field, holding something up in his hand. I couldn't believe my eyes when I realized it was my missing pearl earring.

I looked at him in shock, wondering how on Earth (or off of Earth) he'd found it. I giggled slightly in excitement that my precious, dainty pearl stud had been found and returned to me. After showering him with a hundred thanks, I asked how and when he found the piece of jewelry.

Amazingly, Kenny reported that he'd actually caught it in midair as we were all exiting the plane and had held on to it all the way back down to the ground. It wasn't my altimeter he'd been pointing at, but my missing jewelry!

I was stunned that Kenny the cameraman was able to save such a precious token off mine during that fast-paced, critical moment of the jump. It was almost a miracle that he'd grabbed that tiny article out of thin air while so many other things were going on, and I was so grateful for his help. His job was to help create an unforgettable experience for me, and he'd done that more than once. Not everyone can say their cameraman caught a pearl earring for them in the midst of a free fall – but I can!

Kenny captured some of the smallest, most important details through his video and pictures of my jump. It would have been nearly impossible to take in the entire experience without the digital account of it to review later. I was only off of the ground for a total of thirty minutes. Thanks to Kenny, I am able to relive the best thirty minutes of my life anytime I want, just by popping in a DVD.

I've watched that video over and over again, still in awe of the jump and the finding of the pearl earring. Throughout the entire video, it is visible in Kenny's hand. I reviewed the moment when he grabbed my hand, and the pearl was between his fingers.

He held on to the sentimental trinket for the whole trip down.

This is a story I often tell when encouraging others to give skydiving a try. Many have a hard time believing it actually happened, but Kenny's DVD is all the proof I need. This girl with the pearl earring has been skydiving a few more times since then, and I attribute that urge to such a phenomenal and unique first experience. It wouldn't have been the same without Kenny.

I fly quite a bit, but I never really know what to expect. I seldom disembark from the plane before it lands, but I am glad that this was a whole different kind of plane ride. Since that initial jump, I have gone on three subsequent skydives, and I trained to jump on my own, which was an entirely different experience in itself. For me, it all stems from the first successful attempt. I will be forever grateful for Kenny's generosity that day, not only in rescuing my earring, but for the memory he preserved for me. I will never forget that day.

Chapter Nine

Dr. Curlson, the Romantic Chemist

The summer before I flitted off to college as a bright-eyed undergraduate, the university summoned all incoming freshmen for orientation. The school would be hosting a two-day seminar for students and their parents to learn more about the school, extracurricular activities, and living arrangements for the school year.

There was a detailed agenda, packed with a plethora of items that I wasn't remotely interested in. It was my last summer to hang out and go to the movies with my friends, and I was far too preoccupied to be bothered with a trip to college before I had to be there. I showed the information packet to my mother, and she insisted that I go.

Bloomington, Indiana was only a three-hour drive from where I grew up. My parents and I packed up our stuff and headed down the road. I was a bit jaded about having to attend. Being eighteen and almost a college student, I was sure I already knew everything. My older sister was had attended IU, and she was my go-to person for any questions I had. I rolled my eyes as we started zooming down the highway.

When we arrived at the school, there were banners plastered everywhere, welcoming the incoming freshmen to orientation. We made our way to the hotel first to check in. The service manager handed us an itinerary and directed us to meet the rest of the group in the large auditorium for the opening ceremony at two o'clock in the afternoon.

My parents suggested that we grab a bite to eat beforehand and walk through the campus for a tour so we could get a feel for the place and see where things were located. I complied, and we strolled around the inspiring campus, making our way toward the auditorium.

When we arrived, there were hundreds of students milling around and mingling with one another. I did not know anyone, so I stuck close to my parents. The ushers helped us find three seats so we could sit together. People filed in with their families and filled in the open spots. Soon, the audience was seated and ready for the opening ceremony to begin.

An older man hobbled onto the stage and up to the podium. He had grayish-white hair, and a long beard adorned his face. He wore small, round-framed glasses and conservative attire and was carrying a short stack of papers.

A few people were whispering softly, just enough to make a distraction, but they weren't a disturbance to the presentation.

The man began to address the crowd and started by thanking us all for our attendance. He encouraged people to ask questions as they learned more about the school throughout the course of the weekend. He formally introduced himself, announcing that he was a professor at the university and had worked with thousands of students during his tenure. He'd spent countless hours mentoring students who were looking to create a future.

He frequently met one on one with students to help them plan out their schedules for the following semester. He had a knack for words and delivered them in such a way that he easily captured the attention of the audience. Little did I know that nestled in his speech would be one of the most unforgettable pieces of advice that I would ever hear in my life.

It takes a lot to gain traction in the minds of a group of almost-college students. When a speaker talks to an assembly of young adults, it is vital not only to capture their attention, but also to relate the information that is most vital and applicable to their interests.

Young adults at that age have a relatively short attention span, and speakers use a variety of methods to take advantage of it. The professor chose to use an anecdotal approach in his delivery of the message he wanted to convey. He answered one of the questions every incoming freshman is asked over and over again: "What do you want to do with the rest of your life?" None of the people in that audience could argue with his unique answer.

The professor told us about one of his previous students with whom he'd worked one on one. Like most students, "Brad" had gone to Indiana University looking to build a foundation for the rest of his life. Brad met the professor in one of his classes and looked up to him as a mentor and advisor. He hit the ground running in his college career and earned great grades. Even after Brad completed his four years of college, he stayed in touch with the professor.

The professor told the audience that Brad was now one of the leading chief executive officers (CEO) of a Fortune 500 company. He'd become a well-known leader in his industry, respected by his fellow executives as a knowledge source. As I sat listening to the story, I couldn't help but think it was some sales pitch just to get some of us to sign up for business school. The reputation of the Kelley School of Business is untouched by many other schools, and I was under the impression that the professor was simply trying to persuade new recruits for the program. To my surprise, that was almost the exact opposite of his goal.

Next, the professor asked us to make a guess as to what Brad had majored in at IU. Many people yelled out, "Law! Business! Marketing! Accounting!" and a few other financially based programs, but the professor simply shook his head. He waited a few more minutes before unveiling one of the most unexpected concentrations of study for a prominent CEO. Brad had majored in French horn, of all things!

At first, I almost didn't believe it. *How could the CEO of a Fortune 500 company major in French horn?* we all wondered. The professor smiled at the crowd as everyone let out a chorus of disbelieving sounds. He then confirmed that we'd heard him correctly. The illustrious Brad had spent his undergraduate work at Indiana University studying one of the most graceful of brass instruments. The CEO had been a music student.

Brad's love and devotion to music did not define his future. Rather, it helped to support it. His business aspirations were only enhanced by his degree. The professor's message to us that day was clear: An incoming freshman's choice of major did not matter. A degree in any concentration from such an accredited school offered limitless potential for a student's future. No matter what major a freshman selected, they would not forever be glued to that course of study.

The professor had made sense, and everyone's attention was trained on him. At that young, bright-eyed stage, none of us really knew what we wanted to do when we grew up. We didn't have enough experience to grasp what our futures might hold. Not only did the professor affirm that our indecision was acceptable, but he encouraged us to explore the unknown. Surprisingly, he was the first adult that I heard admit that not knowing exactly what I wanted out of life at this juncture was "ok." According to him, we all deserved the opportunity to try classes outside the normal realm of our comfort zones, for discovering one's goals and aspirations is what college is really all about. I liked his philosophy.

He encouraged us to take risks and said none of us would ever know what we really wanted out of our college career until we dived into subjects with which we were unfamiliar. Even if we chose to start off majoring in French horn, we could ultimately head down a different path. That message resonated and stuck with me.

The professor finished his speech and thanked the audience once again for their decision to join the IU family. Everyone applauded for him at the end of his speech.

After that, it was time to mosey through the rest of the items on the agenda.

The university split the parents and the students in two separate groups to visit various parts of the campus. The parents would focus on the safety of their children, as well as the eating arrangements and study centers – the things parents are most concerned about.

Incoming students, on the other hand, were shuffled off to placement exams to determine their entry levels of study. We also toured the library and dormitories and ended with a meeting with advisors to schedule our first semester of classes. My parents wished me luck and encouraged me to pay attention, and I waved goodbye to them and joined the student group.

Being the social butterfly that I am, I met a few people and discussed the professor's speech with them. Everyone had very positive things to say about it. I agreed and inquired about where they were from. We all took turns introducing ourselves and sharing a little of our background. Some already knew what they were going to study and told us of their majors: "My name is Sally. I'm from Boise, Idaho, and I'm going to major in elementary education. What about you?" Since I was fairly unsure about what was in store for me, I kept it simple and left those details out.

We toured the entire campus and took the required exams for math placement. My high scores earned me a seat in high-level calculus.

Those of us seeking a liberal arts degree also had to select a foreign language. I'd never been extraordinarily fond of learning Spanish, but since I'd taken five years of it from seventh through eleventh grade, I thought that was something I could take care of rather easily. It was still fairly fresh in my mind from high school, and I hoped that knowledge would serve as a foundation for the additional requirements. My grades on that placement test meant I only had to take one semester of it.

The test results were important, because the next stop on our agenda was a meeting with an advisor to schedule our classes for the upcoming term.

I walked into the advisor's office and introduced myself, offering a very grown-up handshake.

She welcomed me to campus and to her office, and offered me a seat in the chair in front of her desk. As I organized my belongings by my feet, she pulled a thick manual from her bookshelf, the class offerings for the upcoming semester. She asked me to pass her my test scores, and after looking them over, she recommended advanced math and Spanish. She then inquired about my choice of major.

I told her I was still unsure about what I really wanted to do, and her reaction was almost identical to the professor who'd spoken to us earlier in the day: She gave me the indication that it was perfectly natural to be so uncertain during the first semester of college.

That put me at ease, and I took the lead in the conversation. Prior to the orientation, my sister and I had read through some of the descriptions for classes that would be beneficial and applicable to almost any selected major. Many of the required electives were general education courses, and I planned to sign up for them for my first semester, while I was gaining a deeper understanding of the specifics that I might want to get into. This was a plan to help me gain my bearings.

Ever the teacher's pet, school was important to me from the get-go. From as early on as elementary school, I considered it my job to be an excellent student. My parents had instilled in me that education would be the key to my future success, and I worked hard throughout the school year to earn grades that would garner pleased reactions from them. No, I didn't get any money for good grades; what I received as a reward was my parents' pride. That was something I understood at a young age, and I longed for them to be pleased in me.

As a kid, I was a devoted student who was very engaged

in my classes, and I enjoyed many of them by the time I reached high school. One class that I truly relished was chemistry. The intricate science of periodic elements, potions, concoctions, and the integration of mathematics was something I found appealing, and it made sense to me. It only helped matters that I had a phenomenal teacher who took the time to explain the concepts thoroughly, so chemistry was something I wanted to study further.

I remembered that during my discussion with my sister about my college courses. I asked her what she thought of taking a basic chemistry course, and she laughed at me. Her forte was journalism, and chemistry couldn't have been further from her interests. She tried to steer me in a different direction by pointing out a few philosophical classes, as she believed they would challenge me to think outside the box. I valued her opinion and her experience and paid heed to her recommendations. After all, she was a veteran of the college life.

There was one particular class with an odd name: Race, Gender, Religion Identity: Who Am I? It sounded very sophisticated, so I thought it would be the perfect opportunity to take her up on her suggestion. It seemed as if it would be a challenge, and I was ready to tackle it as a new college student. I shared that with my advisor, and she nodded to me in approval. I also asked her which basic chemistry course would count toward my requirements, and when she found one that would fit into general education, I signed up.

Once my first-semester courses were chosen, I was ready to become a true college student. Orientation had afforded me with a new outlook on the university, and I felt comfortable about my decision to go there. The summer was waning, and as the days ticked by, I found myself thinking more and more about my would-be adventures at IU. I was apprehensive to meet my professors and classmates, and college seemed so much different than high school. Six weeks after orientation, classes began.

The first day of school in any grade is a bit daunting, whether it's kindergarten or college. I found my class buildings in advance so I would know exactly where to be and wouldn't be late to class. I strolled through campus and passed by hundreds of people I didn't know. When I entered each of my classrooms, it was the same routine. Students would begin trickling in about fifteen minutes before class. Since few of us knew each other, most sat and silently stared, smiling occasionally when others looked back at them.

For the majority of my classes, the process was the same. The professor would walk in and survey the setup of the room.

On that first day, most simply passed out their syllabus and discussed the rules regulations, and policies that would set the standards for the semester. They introduced themselves formally, providing a bit of background information about their time in the academic world, and remarked about their visions for the particular session we were in. Class would wrap up after a total of twenty minutes, with the promise of the second session being more vigorous. Most of the first-day classes required homework in the form of some light reading to prepare for the next session.

Chemistry was my last class of the day, and I figured it would be like all the others. We all entered a large lecture hall and selected a seat, spread out here and there throughout the stadium seating configuration and waiting quietly for the professor to enter. After what seemed like an eternity, he finally arrived.

The professor was a tall, thin man dressed in slacks and a button-down shirt and a tie. From his place in front of the class, he scanned the crowd and offered us a bright, toothy smile. He had black, curly hair styled in a long, shaggy, and there was a charming aura about him. I was sure he couldn't have been any older than thirty. I looked around at my classmates and noticed that I was not the only girl who was blushing in the presence of such an attractive teacher.

Dr. Michael Curlson, as he introduced himself, had a PhD in chemistry, and he mentioned that he was very much looking forward to the semester. I figured he would next go over the do's and don'ts, but instead he just chatted with us. He said he wanted to get to know us better and initiated conversation about our summer, asking if we'd been on any exciting trips and encouraging us to tell him about the best part of the summer and to let him know if anyone had any unique stories to share about the last three months.

A few students shared their memorable summer moments. Some had gone on a last hoorah with their high school buddies, and others had volunteered at local charities. Many had spent their last months of freedom working at summer camps near their hometowns, and others had simply relaxed at home.

When everyone was finished sharing, Dr. Curlson told us all that his summer was one of the most memorable of his life because he'd just proposed to his fiancée. At the mere mention of his significant other, Dr. Curlson beamed with pride. Clearly, the proposal was something he'd been looking forward to for a while. He continued talking without being provoked by anyone, and he was happy to tell us his romantic story. What an introduction it was!

Two years prior to the fall 2004 school year, Dr. Curlson, who was on the brink of becoming a doctor, was traveling to Minneapolis to complete part of his education. He was only there for about a week to attend a few required seminars and was looking forward to his return home. He said he felt tired, groggy, and lethargic as he trekked through the airport. When he finally made it through security and to his gate, there was not much time left over before the call to board.

He waited until his seating arrangement was called and gathered his stuff so he could board the plane. His plan was to relax and catch up on some sleep. He found his assigned seat and noticed a young lady about his age, seated in his row. He placed his items in the overhead compartment, nudged down into his seat, buckled his seatbelt, and halfway listened to the crew's instructions.

As the plane took off, his plan to sleep went awry, for the lady sitting next to him turned out to be quite a conversationalist. When he was telling the class this story, I think I rolled my eyes at his mention of it. I have always been classified that way, and I embrace the ability to carry on a good talk with almost anyone I meet. I consider it to be a rare natural gift.

He and the young lady introduced themselves and chatted for the entire flight about absolutely nothing. To his surprise, it turned out to be the best conversation he ever had. It had far less to do with the meat of their discussion and far more to do with the one who was talking to him.

He was absolutely, almost instantly enamored by her. He described to us her giggle, the way she flipped her hair around as she told stories, and her eyes glistening when a beam of light entered through the airplane window as the plane turned to the right or left.

By that point in his story, the entire class was at attention. Who doesn't enjoy a good love story? I'd walked into class that day anticipating a brief introduction by a cold, boring chemistry professor, followed by a homework assignment, but I got so much more than I'd bargained for!

His flight did not last long enough, in his opinion, and he just knew he had to find a way to contact her after they left the airport. Dr. Curlson was too shy to ask for her phone number, and he explained that it would have been quite awkward to proposition a perfect stranger with a date. We all nodded our heads in agreement to that, for it is the kind of thing that generally only happens in the movies – and even in the greatest of romantic comedies, it seldom works out.

So, they parted company that day without exchanging information. He was disappointed in himself for being such a coward, for she'd had such a great impact on him in such a short period of time. Dr. Curlson decided that he needed to get to know the woman better, but he had no idea how to locate someone he knew virtually nothing about, other than her first and last name and the general vicinity where they both resided. Fortunately, that was all the information the Internet required. Within milliseconds, he had her phone number. "And the rest was history," he said.

We all knew exactly what that meant. He contacted her, and she agreed to a date. His charm, outgoing personality, and early success in life were all alluring to her. He did not delve into much detail about their past two years together, but he was happy to tell us about the summer of his proposal.

They went on a week-long trip to Hawaii before the school year started, a destination they'd both wanted to visit. The sandy beaches, the green palm trees, and the crashing waves would make the perfect backdrop for him to pop the question, and that was exactly where he proposed to the love of his life.

That was the first time I'd ever been in a classroom that had broken out in a round of applause,* and it was a teacher introduction that I would never forget. He'd met his future wife on an airplane just by sitting next to her. He had a far less romantic plan in mind, hoping to sleep without being bothered by any of his noisy neighbors, but when he took the chance to talk to a chatty, friendly young lady, it changed his life forever.

Our chemistry teacher's story resonated with me. He had been randomly seated on that flight – or so it seemed – and ultimately, it enabled him to meet the woman of his dreams. It is difficult to ponder how something so romantic and seemingly happenstance can happen. He gleamed with pride as he told his unique story to the class, and I walked out of chemistry on the first day having learned more in the thirty minutes of introduction than I would learn in some courses all year. (I suppose that could be taken as a bit of an exaggeration, but I will attest to the lesson being far more valuable than some class information I received.)

---

* Many rounds of applause occurred during my undergraduate tenure. Many of the students and professors had the utmost respect for the individuals in classrooms. During compelling lectures, stellar student presentations, and surprise guest appearances, people were so moved that they felt the need to clap. One of my friends even told me about his History of Rock and Roll class, in which the students offered the professor a standing ovation before every session of the course simply because it was that good. I never had the chance to take that course, so I didn't get to experience it myself, but it sounded fantastic.

He chose to offer us a bit of insight into his personal life, and he taught the remainder of the semester in the same, very human way, relying on relatable anecdotes with an emotional appeal to get his point across in a memorable way, even when it came to chemical equations. That made the class interesting and showed that he was not just a professor, but a person. It also reaffirmed my belief that you really never know who you might meet on a plan – or how they might change your life forever!

It has been a goal of mine to challenge myself and take risks every once in a while. Even if it is as simple as taking an introductory chemistry course, the impact can amount to so much more. I didn't end up majoring in chemistry. In fact, that was the one and only time during my college years that I learned a little more about the periodic elements. Nevertheless, I am forever grateful that I ended up choosing that course. Without that speech about Brad's French horn major, I may never have gone in that direction. The message the professor delivered that day was crystal clear.

Chapter Ten

Mark, the Morning Drunk

I finished up a week-long business trip in southern California and was ready to return home. Being so far away, the only reasonable flight that would get me home before sundown required one stopover and an airplane change. The first leg of the flight was relatively short. I set my alarm clock for super early in the morning and prepared for a long day. The end result was that I would get to sleep comfortably in my own bed that night.

It was a Friday, so I assumed travel would be heavy that day with people traveling back home or flying out for a weekend fling. When I got to the airport in the wee hours of the morning, sometime around five thirty a.m., the security line was light. There were a few travelers trekking through the gates that early, but most appeared to be businesspeople. I was still half-asleep, rubbing my tired eyes and yawning incessantly. My flight was scheduled to take off at seven forty a.m.

Although I left time to grab a bite of something to eat in one of the airport cafés, I did not have much of an appetite at that hour. Most of the little shops and kiosks were not even open yet anyway, so I found a comfortable seat near my gate and tore my computer out of my briefcase, figuring the least I could do was get caught up on some work.

The morning was mundane, the same dull routine I'd expected. The airline employee soon called for passengers to start boarding, and I sleepily hobbled over to the line. I blankly stared at my fellow passengers, not registering any of the sights, sounds, or communication that was going on around me. I was too exhausted to comprehend much of anything at all except my flight number being called.

I found my aisle seat on the airplane and settled down into it. The first flight lasted for only about forty-five minutes, so there really wasn't enough time for a nap or to get any work done. My plan was to just sit back and relax a bit.

A young, tattooed man who looked to be about my age took the window seat and put his noise-canceling headphones over his ears. He was dressed in baggy jeans and t-shirt with a Fox Racing logo on it. He appeared to be the quintessential California surfer. At that point, I just turned to pay attention to the other people loading the plane.

For a while, it seemed as if the person assigned to our middle seat was not going to show. It is always a welcomed surprise when that seat remains open, so I was hopeful. The space is already cramped as it is, and the open spot alleviates some of the shuffling of belongings.

Most airlines sell out every seat on their flights to reduce the overhead costs. Any paid seat, despite a high or low price as compared to others, is additional revenue for the ride. After the last person boarded the plane and the seat remained vacant, I felt confident that it might be my lucky day after all.

Flight attendants were helping people find their seats, and during that process, I heard some rustling around behind me in the aisle. I turned around to see what going on and simultaneously, a boisterous, shouting man almost fell into our row. He turned around with a sly, evil grin on his face and announced that he was going to sit in our row. As he put his stuff away, he warned the two of us that he was "loud, chatty, and ready to have a good time." I was immediately disenchanted and annoyed, because none of those things were what I was ready to deal with at seven fifteen in the morning.

As soon as he sat down, I gagged from the foul stench that seemed to be wafting off of him in waves. He reeked like someone who'd been drinking at a bar all night and hadn't had a shower or a toothbrush for days. A faint smell of cigarettes only added to the noxious musk of his odor. I later found out that my predictions were 100 percent accurate. Without provocation, "Mark" introduced himself in an almost taunting way to both me and the guy sitting in the window seat, telling us how much fun we were going to have, while simultaneously cautioning us that people usually did not like sitting by him on airplanes.

Just what the heck am I in for, then, with this smelly, crazy man sitting right by me?

I was reading a book quietly in my seat to pass the time when Mark insisted on interrupting me. He asked what I was reading and made a lewd remark in the process, implying that my book was inappropriate. I gave him a blank stare and a roll of the eyes. I am normally not one to be so unfriendly, but he was clearly trying to make a scene and to get a rise out of me. I knew if I responded to his remarks negatively, it would only fuel his fire and encourage him to continue acting like a rude fool.

When the plane finally took off, I could not have been happier about it. The sooner the flight got moving, the faster I would be able to leave the man's presence. We took off without a hitch and were on our way.

The flight attendants were allowed to get up and move about the cabin at 10,000 feet. As soon as they began to serve drinks, Mark pushed the call light. In all my years of traveling, I cannot remember a time when I've ever pushed it, and I had to wonder what on Earth he could possibly need at that early point in the flight.

When the flight attendant came over and asked what he needed, he began to make blatant, suggestive passes at her. Used to complete idiots during her time with the airline industry, she shrugged it off and asked him again in a firm tone what he needed.

He requested a rum and Coke. My facial expression soured when he said it. It was not even eight o'clock in the morning, and I couldn't even stomach breakfast, let alone an alcoholic drink. Suddenly, I understood Mark's stench.

Mark then began to taunt each and every person in our row and near it. He started with an elderly lady one row ahead of us on the opposite side of the plane, minding her own business in the aisle seat, except when she turned around to look at him several times due to the loud decibel at which he was speaking. It was as if someone had turned the volume button all the way up on his voice. He was utterly distracting and disturbing, acting like a disrespectful adolescent, which he most definitely was not – at least not the adolescent part anyway.

Every time she glared at him, Mark crudely motioned a kiss with his lips and blew it toward the poor woman. He thrived on putting on an obnoxious show of bad manners. When he noticed that she was especially annoyed, he burst forth with an even more vile spectacle than before, making faces at her like a little kid when she turned back around to face the front of the plane. His demeanor was despicable.

I am not the kind of person to start a problem, especially with a fool like the one sitting next to me. Instead, I took this opportunity to ask him questions about himself in an effort to keep him distracted. I did not want his poor behavior reflecting on me as a passenger in any way. Airlines have strict policies, and if any of the authorities onboard had realized he was creating issues and threats, he could have faced legal action. I certainly wanted nothing to do with him or the consequences of his rude behavior.

I began my questionnaire with something simple to provoke further discussion. The honest truth was, I couldn't have cared less about the childish man, but I had never seen such outlandish behavior before on a plane from a thirty-something adult male. I was sure my inquisition would help to defuse the situation. I asked him why he was on the flight and where he was going, and his answer was a bit awkward.

Mark told me he was heading to Indianapolis to tend to some property he'd recently acquired. When I probed a bit further, he explained that his best childhood friend, also in his thirties, had just passed away from terminal cancer, leaving behind a wife and children in Indiana. When his friend was alive, he'd earned his living by renting out properties in the greater Indianapolis area, and after he died, the property management had been left in Mark's questionably capable hands. Thus, Mark was heading across the country to sort out all of the rental agreements with the tenants.

When I showed sympathy for the mention of his dead friend, he just creepily laughed and nonchalantly said it wasn't a big deal. "Part of life," he said. "We expected it to happen."

I wondered if he was being serious or just trying to hide the emotional pain of such a tragedy. He'd already obviously tried to drown it.

Death is always difficult to cope with, but in our thirties, our lives are supposed to be flourishing with date nights, kids' soccer games, and lavish dinners with old friends. Death was not a normal part of life Mark's friend, not at such a young age. Surely, his wife and children were at a loss as to how to move on after such a tragic, untimely loss, and Mark was flying in for the rescue.

I suspected that he was covering his pain from the loss of his best friend by pretending to not be upset. His reaction to the situation was difficult to gage, though, as I chatted with him more. He seemed absolutely removed from emotional ties with anyone, almost inhumanly so. Aware that people deal with death in their own unique way, I refrained from nagging him for more information. I had never experienced the death of a young friend, so my sympathetic understanding only stretched so far.

Mark rambled on about his life, and I gave him the floor. My ultimate goal was to keep him from pestering other passengers, and it seemed to be working, because he had no problem talking about himself.

He took a large gulp from the pungent drink in his hand and continued the story. He told me he'd gone to his nightclub the previous night and had drunk it up until three a.m. He then went home to pack his belongings and headed straight to the airport; that explained the fermented scent of his breath and seeping from his pores. He reported that it was "just a "typical Thursday night" for him, and he found it quite an inconvenience to have to alter his plans to go to Indianapolis.

The more Mark divulged, the wider my eyes grew. I should have been able to predict the answer to my next question by that point, but I chose to ask it anyway: "Do you see a girlfriend or a wife in your future, Mark?"

At the mention of a significant other, Mark chuckled with amusement. The thought of sharing his life with another human being obviously repulsed him. He admitted that he was too selfish to spend time with another person and claimed he was "incapable of loving anybody."

I rolled my eyes and didn't try to hide it from him, not caring what he thought of my rude, dismissive gesture. I had to press him on the issue, try to call his bluff, so I asked, "Don't you love your parents?" It seemed like a given to me, but I was wrong again.

This time, Mark just gave me a look and took another big gulp of his toxic beverage. He stared at me for a few seconds before beginning his reply, then turned to me and said flatly, "I don't talk to my mother."

Mark's mom lived only one hour north of his home, but she had demanded that he get his drinking under control before she would talk to him again. He admitted that he thought she was crazy and did not understand what he was going through, but both parties had agreed that an amicable relationship meant not having one at all. Mark didn't even mention his father, which indicated some sort of traumatic absence in his life. His description of his relationship with his mother was foul enough for both parents.

Having always been so close with both of my parents throughout my lifetime, I couldn't imagine not having a relationship with them. Mark's mother lived just one hour from where he was located, yet they refused to see one another. When I lived about two hours away from my parents' house, I drove home just to attend a family dinner night every week. I didn't even think twice about it.

That was like a flashing red light at a four-way intersection. His mother was telling him to stop, look around, and proceed with caution only. If he'd have put himself in her shoes, his perspective would have been skewed. His nonchalant attitude toward being an invisible son in her life was disheartening. From the way he described her, I assumed that she wanted to help him. She clearly recognized that he had a problem. Instead of engaging with her and working as a team to get his life under control, he swore off her love. In his opinion, his mother was the root of the problem and just failed to recognize it.

I momentarily felt sorry for both of them, albeit for different reasons. I pitied him because he could not fathom that the irreparable damage he was doing was truly his fault. Humility and the ability to recognize when one is wrong are key characteristics of integrity. My first impression was that he lacked those qualities altogether. I felt bad for his mother as well; despite her pleas and offering of kindness, the situation was out of her control. Her son was a grown man, and he had to make his own decisions.

Some of his answers helped me piece together Mark's behavior. He was wildly unhappy. He never outright said it in so many words, but I could see it in his eyes when he spoke. An adult who outwardly makes fun of people and needs to be the center of attention in a group of total strangers cannot function properly in society. Those juvenile antics were a desperate cry for others to notice him.

His lack of etiquette was absolutely obnoxious, and I had never seen any adult act that way before, except, perhaps, in a nightclub or bar after a few too many. I did not know whether to blame his behavior on the alcohol or his personality; I concluded it was a nasty combination of both. Since the mention of human relationships seemed so deplorable to him in any form, I pressed the issue further. I persisted with questions regarding siblings, and he cackled before he answered me.

Mark said he had an older sister and a younger brother. Both of them were married with children, but neither wanted anything to do with their brother. Once again, he blamed his grudges, problems, and negativity on them. They wouldn't let him spend time with their kids. They celebrated holidays without inviting him to the parties. They talked about him with their mother behind his back. It was all about him, and it was easy to see that Mark was a very selfish person indeed.

I noticed an overarching pattern in every question he answered: Nothing was ever his fault. He took no responsibility for his actions with or toward others. That had been blatantly obvious from the first moment he plopped down next to me in the seat. As I listened to all of his blaming and unwarranted excuses, I shook my head at him in disbelief.

A moment later, the young fellow sitting near the window seemed to have developed an interest in our conversation. When Mark saw the reaction from his other seatmate, he shouted a question at the guy, sure the California surfer boy would agree with him and take his side. "Hey, you're a younger guy like me. Don't you just wanna party all the time, unlike Debbie Downer over here? Look at her, reading her boring, lame books and gabbing nonstop about her family."

The surfer's response couldn't have been more perfect. He replied that he was flying to visit and spend time with his girlfriend's family. He also told Mark in no uncertain terms that once someone leaves college, it's time to grow up and act like an adult, just as he was doing himself.

The surfer boy went on to explain that he was on the brink of asking his girlfriend to marry him, and the final step before the proposal was to do the honorable thing and ask her parents. He was thrilled to have the opportunity to travel to see them and said his girlfriend had changed his life. They'd met upon their college graduation, and he knew instantaneously that they were soul mates. They supported one another in their individual endeavors and embarked on many new adventures together. The surfer described their relationship as if it was flawless.

I thought Mark was going to throw up as he heard their love story unfold. The scowl on his face articulated his unspoken detest. Mark was flabbergasted to hear it coming from someone his own age. The surfer knew his opposition was irritating Mark, but he spoke from the heart and couldn't have cared less. I ignored Mark's name-calling and relished in the splendor and sincerity of the surfer's story.

Just in the nick of time, the pilot announced that we were beginning our initial descent and should all prepare for landing. The timing on this announcement could not have been more perfect. Mark finally shut up, sulking in his chair in disbelief. The flight attendants circled through the cabin once more to pick up the leftover garbage from the in-flight service. As they approached our row, Mark pouted at the flight attendant like a kid and refused to give up his drink. Unwilling to fight with him, she pretended not to see he still had it. The surfer, on the other hand, handed her the garbage and gleefully thanked her for the help.

The two people sitting in my row were vastly different. One had the ability to love and believed in it wholeheartedly. He was gracious for whatever help people offered him. The surfer cherished time spent with friends and family. Though he didn't say much, the words he did share on the airplane were pure of heart and grateful. I'm not sure why he chose to answer Mark's crazy questions in the first place, but I was glad he did. His answers served to reinforce my assumptions about relationships, life, and love.

Initially, my responses to Mark were somewhat negative. I did not want to hear his sob story or his rants about how much he disliked people. When I contemplated the situation after I left the airport, I changed my perspective. Fate had seated me next to him on the airplane that day for a reason.

My attitude about relationships with people is almost the polar opposite of Mark's. When we were children, my parents made sure my sister and I were involved in social situations with our family and friends. To me, spending time with the people I love is normal. Since it has always been part of our routine, I never gave it a second thought – until I sat next to Mark.

Mark's unrelenting babble about the menial value of people was depressing. I wondered what could have impacted his life in such a negative way that he would act in that manner and have that kind of attitude. Mark's unhappiness fed his addiction to alcohol, not the other way around. The liquor was his vice to curb his depression and make it tolerable. Mark could not function like an adult in public. His outlandish behavior on the flight was a direct reflection of that. His demeanor was rude, and that drove him to push the people who potentially cared about him out of his life. Mark's negativity helped me to appreciate the people I loved so much more.

To Mark, people were just other beings whom he was forced to share the planet with. For me, the people I care about make my life. I can't imagine not being able to chat with my friends and gather around the dinner table to tell old, funny stories with my family. Each person has helped me to create memories that I will forever carry with me, and I cherish the time I have with them.

Although I appreciate my friends and family, I know there is always room to improve my demeanor toward them. Mark and his lack of zest for life encouraged me to do so. It is humbling to be gracious for all that people do for you, no matter how large or small the gesture might be.

As I sat with Mark on the flight, I was proud to have the mental ability to love others and form and nurture real, honest, mutually beneficial relationships with them. I wanted to boast about how incredible each and every person in my life is. Instead, I listened to him and reflected back upon what he said. He didn't have a family, friends, or a significant other to rely on, but I literally can't imagine life without mine. Although it is not likely to occur, I hope Mark finds bliss in his passion in the future. I can only hope he learns to let people into his heart to share in his happiness and he in theirs.

The world is a better place because of the people who are in it. I thrive on the support and encouragement of those people who care about my wellbeing. I was quite lucky to be dealt a hand of some of the world's best. I know this because I have reminders all around me.

Chapter Eleven

Estelle, the Tattooed Actress

Since my boyfriend and I had started dating, I'd been nagging him to take me on a trip to meet his parents. He grew up in a suburb of Kansas City, Missouri. His parents, grandparents, siblings, and cousins were all still in that area, and I was dying to meet all of them. He and I planned events with my family almost weekly, since they lived within a twenty-mile radius of our place, but I had yet to meet his.

Our relationship was progressing, and as it grew more serious, spending time with his family became more of a priority for me. I was curious to explore his roots. He always promised we could visit anytime we wanted, and all I'd have to do would be to book the flight. It seemed simple enough, so I took his advice and did just that one weekend.

We made a joint phone call to his parents the next night to let them know we were going to head out to see them, and I was beyond enthusiastic. I couldn't wait to see his hometown, meet his family, hang out with his childhood friends, and eat delicious homemade food.

When the weekend finally arrived, we decided to meet

at our home and drive together to the airport. After work, I raced back to our house, where he was waiting for me. I'd packed everything up the night before and had calculated the amount of time we would need to get to the airport. We were right on schedule, according to my plan. As we left, I took a deep breath and asked him to tell me about his day at work, hoping that might calm my nerves as we headed down the road.

There were two semi-direct routes that led to the airport from our house. Coincidentally, my boyfriend believed one route was more efficient, and I had the same feelings about the other. He was driving, so we ended up taking his route. It was a Friday evening just before dusk, and the city was booming. Chicago is infamous for horrendous freeway backups, and that night was no exception. As he weaved in and out of traffic, I grew more and more impatient with the process. Assuming that my preferred route was invariably better, I snickered at him. We were at risk to miss our flight, and I was irritated. We bickered back and forth a bit as we continued to slowly crawl toward the airport.

When we eventually arrived in the parking lot, we jumped out of the car like bats bursting out of a cave. We each grabbed our respective luggage and walked toward the shuttle. Once it rolled around, we hopped on and headed to the departure terminal. On approach, I could see the lengthy security lines that awaited us. I glanced at my cell phone to determine how much time we had to spare, and it was not much. We were definitely cutting it close.

We ended up jogging toward our gate, which just so happened to be the very last one in the elongated terminal. Both of us were out of breath by the time we got there. As we approached the podium, the boarding process was in its final stages. We handed our boarding passes for scanning and, once we had clearance, walked toward to terminal.

We boarded to find the entire aircraft full. There were two open middle seats left, and they had our names on them. Regardless of where I sat, I would be crunched between two perfect strangers. I scoped out an opening to my right. An older, well-dressed gentlemen sitting in the aisle seat smiled at me. There was a warm, elderly woman in the window seat. They simultaneously told me they had saved the seat just for me. I placed my belongings under the seat in front of me and sat down.

I glanced up toward where Joe was sitting. The rear of his head poked out of a middle seat about ten rows in front of mine. He put on his noise-canceling headphones and never looked back.

I settled into my chair and buckled myself in. I must have appeared flustered from all the rushing, because the man sitting next to me asked if I was running late. He was quite observant. I slyly smiled over at him and nodded my head. That opened a can of worms, and I began to rant about our hectic drive to the airport. I even divulged our weekend plans to meet my boyfriend's family. Then I introduced myself to the two people sitting next to me.

The man told me his name was "Bernie," and the woman was his "beautiful wife Estelle." They'd been married for forty-one years. The two were on the way home from a trip to Florida to visit their daughter, son-in-law, and two grandchildren. Estelle beamed with pride when her husband described her extended and still growing family. When I turned toward Estelle to shake her hand, I could not help but notice the massive rock she was wearing on her finger. The diamond had to be at least three and a half carats. I'm not a jeweler, but I knew such a stone had to be a rare bauble indeed. Not every day do I sit next to someone with such a public display of wealth on their finger, and I was intrigued.

I glanced up at her face, which I'd been far too self-involved and flustered to enjoy prior to that moment, and realized how flawlessly perfect her makeup was. The black eyeliner had been applied with such precision, such intricate detail that it looked laser cut. Her eyebrows were perfectly sculpted, not one single hair out of place. Her cheeks were warm, rosy blushes, as if she'd just stepped into a warm house from the cold.

Being a woman who does not spend an exorbitant amount of time on makeup application, I was impressed. Whenever I try to add color to my own face, I tend to paint my features on with shaky hands, as if it's impossible to remain still. Thus, I had a hard time believing such an elderly lady would have been able to do so with such precision.

I began my conversation by complimenting her makeup. I told her how perfect she looked and joked about my lack of skills in that regard. She began to giggle, then took the opportunity to reveal the most vital and unusual beauty secret: She was not wearing any makeup at all! I was confused by that at first because her face had so much perfect, complementary color to it, perfectly highlighting her facial features.

Estelle referred to me as "honey" even after I introduced myself by name. It was an endearing, matronly nickname for the duration of our short flight. "You see, honey, when you get older, things don't look like they used to. I never wanted to bother with remembering to put on makeup. I was too busy taking care of the little ones, so I had all my color tattooed on! That was one of my adventures while I was in Florida – just a touch-up."

It was such a shock. I'd never heard of anyone having such a procedure done. I was sure it must have been a painful process around the sensitive areas of her face. Once she revealed her secret, I noticed just how perfect it was. She pointed out the parts that had changed since her last application of ink.

Estelle was a perfectionist. She wanted to look her best at any given time and found a way to do so with minimal daily time commitment. That candid conversation about a somewhat personal topic opened up the beginning to the story of her life. The flawlessness of her face had started way back when she was a young lady. She was unique, but not just because her makeup was tattooed on.

When Estelle was growing up in the 1920s, she'd always dreamt of becoming famous. Her mother signed her up for dance lessons in the small town where they lived. Estelle was young and picked up on the moves from her instructor quickly. She joked about not having the patience or concentration as an adult that she did as a child, but she was always determined to be the best.

Her parents were strict, and since they were paying "good money," as she described it, for her lessons, they expected her to practice. She would dance around her house, outside in the yard, and in the bedroom she shared with her younger sister. As she aged a bit, Estelle became increasingly better and found herself following bigger dreams.

The more she practiced, the better she got. She found herself thinking about auditioning for Broadway and made the decision to follow through with it. She told me it had always been her wish to dance in front of large crowds. She wanted the experience of giving joy to the audience, and she was eager to hear the roar of applause after a stellar performance. That was what got her adrenaline going.

As she told me all of this and reminisced about the past, she actually rolled her eyes back in her head in ecstasy, as if she was reliving her favorite moments simply by retelling the stories. She chuckled at certain parts, basking in the glory of her younger life. I could tell she felt nostalgic over that special time in her career and life.

When she was nineteen, she and a group of her dancing friends headed to New York City. She claimed she auditioned for hundreds of shows and only earned a few small, back-up roles. She learned the choreography with exact precision and grace, and although she did not initially earn a starring role, Estelle expressed to me that it all led up to what she believed was her destiny.

I noticed that her husband kept looking over from the aisle seat, giving her warm, comforting smiles. He loved the happiness he saw on her face when she reminisced about her glory days.

Estelle's dancing continued to improve, and over the years she met hundreds of dancers, performers, and actors she'd admired for most of her life. She found it inspiring to work with those who were more experienced than her, and she learned a lot from them. To keep up with them, she had to practice nonstop, and the additional time she spent perfecting her moves were well worth it.

Estelle recounted that there was a call-out for a Broadway show that would be choreographed by the famous Gene Kelly. She was nervous about working for one of the most famous dancers in history, but she took the time to learn the moves to try out for the part. Estelle practiced for hours on end. When the day arrived, she stepped onto the stage and felt quite empowered. She stood alone on the platform with an audience of a few people staring back at her, but she was ready. She greeted them, introduced herself, and thanked them for their hospitality for hosting her, and then the music commenced.

When Estelle described the way she moved around the stage, her eyes lit up. She told me she felt like she was "floating." Everything felt surreal to her. In a sweet, engaging voice, she recalled that she was completely confident in that performance, perhaps more so than any other she'd ever danced. The small audience clapped after she was finished, then graciously thanked her for the time she'd committed to the routine and indicated that she would find out the results later that week.

Then, in a matriarchal attempt to relate to me, Estelle asked if I had ever anticipated big news that would somehow determine my future. Right away, a memory flashed through my thoughts: my submission into my undergraduate program at Indiana University.

I was a junior in high school when I began to apply for college. The amount of paperwork was overwhelming. Being inexperienced and unfamiliar with the necessary information, I struggled to remain organized.

My parents encouraged me to apply to multiple schools to explore my options, but I disregarded their suggestions. My heart was set on Indiana University, so I made it a priority to do whatever it took to earn my admission to the school. The personal statement I wrote was revised and edited countless times. The references I contacted provided detailed accounts of my achievements. I put forth extra effort to ensure that all paperwork would be turned in on time. The deadline approached, but my submission was complete. I'd given it my all, my best performance, and at that point, just like Estelle, I had to play the waiting game.

The date of notification would be dependent on when application materials were turned in. Being the antsy person I am, I could not wait my turn. The anticipation of my future was overpowering. It felt as if my entire existence hinged on a one-word answer from IU: I desperately wanted – needed – that answer to be "Yes."

Believe it or not, for the most part, students are still informed about their college admissions by formal letter through snail mail. The university sends a letter of acceptance or rejection, along with the proper instructions and next steps that should be taken.

As the date neared for me to learn my fate, I impatiently jumped the gun a little and picked up the phone to call the registrar's office. When a woman answered, I hurriedly introduced myself and explained the reason for my call: "Hello. My name is Kersten Kelly, and I applied to the school a little over a month ago. I am calling to find out the status of my application."

The woman on the other end of the phone asked me to hold so she could rummage through the notes on her computer. After a few minutes, she returned to the phone and asked if I was still there. I indicated that I was, and she said she was happy to report that I was admitted for the freshman class, beginning in fall of 2004.

I leapt three feet into the air in my parents' kitchen and continued to jump up and down. I yelped, screamed, laughed, and cheered into the poor woman's ear, forgetting that she was still on the other end of the phone. I had gotten into my dream school, and I couldn't contain my joy.

As I recalled that, I knew exactly how Estelle felt about her audition. She danced with precise skills in front of the producers and choreographers. It was up to them to determine if her style, flair, and ability were on par with the other performers in the group. As she told the remainder of the story, her eyes lit up like fireworks on the Fourth of July. Estelle earned a small role in the show to dance alongside Gene Kelly.[*]

Her achievement was significant, and she knew it. She was not vain about it, but the self-confidence she'd gained from that experience was apparent, even all those years later. She earned acceptance into an elite group of dancers who would have the rare opportunity to perform with world-renowned artists.

I admired her determination and courage and congratulated her. It had to have been a life-changing moment for her, one that would define her future and her career.

Bernie reaffirmed Estelle's claims and nodded in approval. When the flight attendants came around to ask for drink orders, both Bernie and Estelle ordered gin and tonic. They insisted that I have a drink with them to enjoy the flight a little more. I humbly obliged, and the three of us continued talking, like a group of old friends who'd bellied up to the bar.

My next question was to find out the origins of that huge diamond on her finger. I complimented Estelle on her jewelry and told her how stunningly beautiful and sparkly it was, though I'm sure she already knew that. The brilliance of the glistening rock could be seen from a mile away.

Bernie leaned over and jokingly said, "She *earned* that!" I chuckled a little and asked him to explain.

Bernie and Estelle told the story together. Forty-one years prior, Bernie and Estelle were married in a Chicago church. About a hundred of their closest friends and relatives attended the ceremony and shared that very special day with them. She said she remembered it "like it was yesterday," and Bernie teased that he couldn't understand why she'd agreed to marry him in the first place, though he was glad she did. The two were so inviting

---

[*]   Gene Kelly is most well noted and remembered for his stellar dancing. He also dabbled in choreography, film direction, acting, and singing and produced a variety of programs. He is most well-known for his involvement in *Singin' in the Rain* and *An American in Paris*. He won numerous awards and is a legacy in the performance industry, particularly in New York City.

to talk to, and Bernie's sense of humor was to die for.

Bernie explained the sweet story of how they met. His parents knew Estelle's family very well, for they'd been friends for a very long time. Bernie admitted he'd always "had an eye on her," but Estelle's father would not allow her to date until she was sixteen years old. Estelle piped in that she never thought of Bernie as anything more than the annoying son of her father's friend. I laughed at that, and the story went on.

On Estelle's sixteenth birthday, Bernie asked her to the soda shop for ice cream, a customary way to court in those days. And, as they say, the rest was history. It sounded way too good to be true, and I didn't even know what a soda shop was. They laughed at me and at themselves, admitting that they were really showing their age.

A year ago, the couple had celebrated their fortieth wedding anniversary. To make the milestone memorable, Bernie bought that astounding diamond ring for Estelle.

I congratulated them on the depth of their love and the length of their marriage. My parents celebrated their thirty-fourth wedding anniversary in 2012, and I have witnessed the same commitment, patience, and compromise in them that I saw in Estelle and Bernie. A marriage cannot last that long without those qualities. The best part was that Estelle and Bernie still acted like newlyweds. When she spoke, he acted as if her voice was an orchestra of beautiful instruments. I was happy for them and happy that such love could still exist in the world.

The flight to Kansas City did not last long. It was just a little over an hour, but it felt like five minutes. Estelle and Bernie were not only unique, but also memorable. The ring and tattoos were interesting, but the deeper meaning behind the relationship they shared was everlasting. They gave me the reassurance and confidence to trust in love, friendship, companionship, and dreams – all the values that are vital to happiness for me and everyone else.

Chapter Twelve

Saint Anthony, the Lucky Finder

When I was a little kid, I used to beg my parents to tell me stories. The actual stories themselves were really irrelevant; what was truly important was the chance to steal my mother's or father's undivided attention for twenty minutes as they regaled me with one of their memories. I have a list of favorites that were told over and over again, and I never got sick of them. Some of the stories stuck out more than others. One, in particular, was the story of my mother's prayer to St. Anthony.

My mother grew up in a large family, the second oldest of four children. Her father was a bricklayer and worked long days and sometimes even nights to provide for the family. My grandmother was a nurse, but she always made sure to spend ample time at home with her children and always made sure there was a meal on the table every night. When the family was finished eating, she even found time and energy to clear the dishes away to the kitchen.

My mother often helped her mother clean up the dinner mess. Because the luxury of dishwashers was nonexistent during that time, the piles of dishes, pots, and pans had to be washed and dried by hand. Since this was a nightly routine, my mother became good at it and became comfortable in the routine.

Before putting their hands in the soapy water, my mom and grandma would take off their rings and place them on the ledge above the sink to prevent the dishwater from dulling the gold and the stones. One night after all the dishes were washed and dried, my mom went to grab the brand new ring her boyfriend had given her. When she reached over the ledge to pick it up, it was gone.

My mom described her initial reaction as panic. She began to frantically search around the area and, without any reservations, plunged her hand into the dirty, greasy dishwater to the bottom of the sink where all of the rotten food had settled. She felt around in the greasy, soapy water and the debris and tidbits left over from the evening's cuisine.

When she didn't find the ring there, she began to crawl around on the kitchen floor, looking under cabinets and churning up occasional dust-bunnies and food particles. She ventured back over to the dinner table, trying to recall the exact moment when she'd taken it off her finger, trying to retrace her steps. No matter where she looked, there was no sign of her ring. With a fear-stricken face, she asked her mother about it, and to my mother's horror, she hadn't seen it either.

For the next four days, she searched everywhere. She tore apart every cabinet, taking out all of the dishes and restocking them only after she'd made absolutely sure there was no trace of the trinket. She rummaged through her bedroom, looking under the mattress, between the sheets, and through her dresser drawers. She was on a mission, determined to find that lost piece of beloved jewelry, a token of her boyfriend's love for her.

When the search in her house failed, she moved her hunt outside to the alley in back of her parents' garage. She had no idea how it would have gotten out there, but she had to look everywhere. The ring couldn't have just disappeared into thin air.

Her parents lived on the south side of Chicago, and the alleys lining the back yards were filthy. She approached the massive garbage cans with caution, attempting to avoid the maggots that thrived on morsels of decaying food. She began to dig out full garbage bags and ripped them open, ignoring the stench and trying to locate her precious ring. The odor protruding from the garbage was putrid, causing my mom to gag every few seconds. She disregarded her sensory reactions, though, and continued her search. My mom pulled every piece of trash out of the can but still found no ring among the rubbish.

Feeling defeated and deflated and depressed from the fruitless search, she went back into the house. Her heart was broken, for the symbol of affection from her boyfriend was missing. She didn't know what she was going to tell him.

My grandma noticed the sadness on my mother's face and had a suggestion for her: "Pray to St. Anthony."

I am not an overly religious person, but as I child, I was intrigued to hear any story that included even a shred of anything that seemed magical. I wanted to know what made that saint so special that he would be able to help her find the ring. My mother explained that in the Catholic religion, St. Anthony is the spirit one prays to when something is lost; in fact, that is the premise behind the common saying, "Tony, Tony, look around. Something's lost and must be found."

My mother was desperate and willing to try anything, so she knelt down next to her bed and said a prayer to St. Anthony, begging for his help. She then went about the rest of her day.

The next morning, she awoke, naturally still thinking about her ring. Since it had been a few days since she'd last seen it, and she'd looked everywhere she could possibly think of and had asked everyone about it, she could only assume that the ring was gone forever. As she contemplated how she was going to break the grim news to her boyfriend, she was overcome with a sudden urge to go outside and look in the trash again. She said she did not know why, but she was somehow unavoidably compelled to get out of bed and go look outside, dressed in only her pajamas.

Since she'd already gone through all of the trash, she was sure this repeat effort was going to be in vain. Insects were swarming around everywhere, feasting on the stinky remains, and the decaying trash was oozing out of the bags. The trashcan itself was filthy. She pulled the garbage bags out one by one, until she reached the bottom of the can. She gasped when she saw the small item that she'd been seeking for so long. There was her ring, sitting right in the bottom of the trashcan, drowning in filth and grime. Amazingly, the jewels were sparkling and perfectly clean. The jewelry was unharmed and looked almost brand new.

My mother was beside herself with emotion and happiness that her ring was finally back in her possession. The shock wore off after a bit, and she didn't even have to tell her boyfriend that his gift to her had gone missing temporarily.

I heard that story countless times as a young person, but it really never got old. I took it for a miracle, but I was never really convinced St. Anthony had much to do with it. It was only a single incident, after all.

My mom must be prone to losing important jewelry at inopportune times. A few years ago, while on vacation, a similar incident occurred. My parents insisted on arriving at the airport with more than enough time to spare before their flight (a trait I likely inherited from them). My mom had planned the day meticulously, leaving them enough time to grab a bite to eat before takeoff. They milled through security and searched for a comfortable spot to sit down.

When they found a row of fast-food eateries, my mom plopped down on the seat and kept the bags company while my father trekked to the counter to order their gourmet, deep-fried meal. They described the atmosphere as very relaxing, quite dissimilar to the chaos I usually face at the airport these days. The two of them enjoyed watching various passengers race through the busy intersections and chitchatted about the people they were watching.

Once they were finished eating, my mother indicated that she needed to use the restroom. She scurried off to the side of the terminal while my father waited for her. A few minutes later, she accompanied Dad to their assigned gate.

My parents sought out a set of adjoining seats in which to rest before the boarding process began. They settled into the area and removed some of the bags that were dangling from their shoulders. As they did that, my dad shot a perplexed facial expression in my mother's direction. Being the perceptive person that she is, she noticed his look right away. She sneered back at him and asked what the face was all about. Much to my mother's dismay, he explained that the diamond pendant hanging from her neck was no longer holding a diamond.

My mother described her feelings that day as the same ones she'd felt on that fateful day as a teenager, when her ring came up missing after the dishwashing. Her stomach dropped to her knees, and a wave of warmth circulated through her blood. Her body nonverbally communicated her stress, for one of the most sentimental symbols of love my father had ever given her had vanished when the pendant prongs had let loose of their precious stone. With a ticking clock on the departure of their flight, she had to strategize a plan immediately. There wasn't any time to waste if she ever wanted to see her jewel again.

As long as I can remember, my mother has always overreacted in stressful situations. Her response in this situation was no different. She babbled on and on about how horrible she felt for losing it.

My father, on the other hand, remained relatively composed, as he considers jewelry and other material things to be replaceable. He has never allowed himself to become emotionally attached to trinkets. Therefore, he responded to my mother's outburst with dignity and restraint. His sole purpose was to calm her down. He promised that if she did not find it, they could pick out a new one.

She ignored his suggestion as if he were crazy. She was bound and determined to repeat her jewelry luck another time.

In my father's attempt to settle my mom down, he calmly suggested that she retrace her steps. She agreed to the plan and started babbling aloud about where she'd been. She told my dad she would be back in a few minutes and to call her on her cell phone if he happened to find it. The plan was to meet regardless of the search results when boarding began at their gate, and that didn't leave them much time.

My mom trekked back to the food court where they had eaten their lunch. The gem could have been anywhere, and she assumed she might have inadvertently, unknowingly thrown it away with the pile of soft white napkins or wrapped it up in the paper that had held her burger.

By the time she got back there, another couple had already seated themselves at that table. Paying no mind to the lack of etiquette or politeness, she interrupted their meal to ask them if they would get up so she could look under the table. When she explained the situation, they were more than happy to abide by her request. She ducked to the dirty, food-littered floor, but she saw nothing glistening down there.

After thanking the couple for their kind compliance, she hurried over to the restroom. She remembered combing her hair over the sink after she washed her hands. She went over to the basins to skim the tile that lined the floor under them. She moved from left to right, carefully keeping her eye out for the slightest sparkle. Some of the bathroom attendants and other travelers questioned what she was looking for. When she described her dilemma, they kindly helped her search. Unfortunately, even with all those sets of eyes, no one was able to locate her precious stone.

Time was running out for my mother, and she felt defeated all over again. As she was walking back to the gate in utter disappointment, she remembered something: This time, she hadn't bothered to pray to St. Anthony. In her mind, she made a solemn request to the spirit to help her pinpoint where her charm had wandered off to. As she did so, the thought struck her that there were only forty-five minutes left before her flight was scheduled to leave.

She found my father sitting at the gate; he hadn't had any luck finding the gem either. She told him she'd looked under the table and in the restroom and had even enlisted the help of others, all to no avail. My father listened and tried to console his wife, promising that they would replace the gem with a newer, even shinier one as soon as the trip was over.

As Dad continued comforting her with positive affirmations, my mother was suddenly struck with an odd urge to look in the bathroom again, specifically under the sinks. She interrupted my father to tell him she'd be right back.

He barely got the chance to respond before scurried off. When she entered the bathroom, she looked down toward the tile. There were new patrons in the bathroom by then, and they quickly realized the poor woman was frantically searching for something on the ground. As she weaved up and down the lines of tile, something suddenly caught her eye. There was her diamond, glistening on the ground as if surrounded by an aura all its own, courtesy of the reflection from the fluorescent lighting.

Mom hurled herself down beside the gem and scooped it up. She literally screamed, "My diamond! I found my diamond!" to a crowd of complete strangers in the ladies' room. Everyone clapped, as they could sympathize with her situation. The tension in her body immediately eased, and she trotted proudly and victoriously back to the gate, where my father was waiting for her.

My dad rolled his eyes when he saw the ear-to-ear grin across her face. He was shocked that she'd retrieved the diamond off the floor just in the nick of time, and they boarded their flight without any issues.

To this day, my mother argues that it was the prayer to St. Anthony that helped her find her precious treasures. I will never understand how either piece of jewelry showed up after such a vigorous search had proven unfruitful, but it seems to presumptive to think it happened – twice – by mere coincidence. Whether it was the result of prayer or some astounding good luck, my mother could now fully enjoy her trip.

One of my many adventures on an airplane led me to rethink this story. It was August of 2012, and I was on a business trip for work. I made it through security in record time, and since I hate using the facilities in flight, I made a quick stop in the restroom before trekking to my gate. As I was washing my hands, I noticed a tiny ring on the ledge next to the sinks. There was no one else in the restroom, so I picked the ring up to have a better look at it.

At first glance, it did not appear to be anything special. There were several miniscule diamonds outlining the outside of it, and a row of sapphires in the middle added a soft blue glow. It looked to be silver or white gold. I presumed someone had taken it off to wash her hands, much like my mother did when she washed dishes so long ago.

Clearly, the ring had been forgotten and left there, quite possibly because the traveler was in a hurry. I initially assumed it was someone from Chicago, but it struck me that it was a ludicrous thought, since the airport was a stopping point for people from all over the world. That piece of jewelry could have belonged to *anyone*.

From the looks of it, it didn't seem to be worth much from a monetary standpoint. It was too simple, and the stones were small and seemingly insignificant. I wondered how long it would take the poor woman to realize it wasn't on her finger. I contemplated just leaving the ring in the bathroom in case she thought to come back and look for it, but I feared a dishonest person might play finders-keepers with it.

As thoughts rambled through my head as to what I should do that might help the ring reconnect with its owner, I glanced down at my own fingers. On my right hand, I wear a vintage yellow gold ring with sixteen marquee diamonds lined in two separate rows, a bauble from the 1930s, with an antique flair to it. I have yet to find a replica with the precision and intricate detail of my band. It belonged to my late grandmother and was a gift left for me in her passing. The sentimental, heartfelt significance of that ring far superseded any dollar value, and I would be devastated if it ever went missing, as it is the only piece of my dear grandmother that I have left.

On my left hand, I wear the most beautiful piece of jewelry

I have ever seen, an engagement ring adorned with a round-cut center diamond on a solitaire band. It beautifully symbolizes the love my fiancé and I share, as well as the beginning of the rest of our lives together. Anytime I need a reminder of how wonderful my life is, I look down at both of my hands and cherish the individuals I care about so much. Not ever wanting to take that feeling away from another person, I knew what I had to do with the ring.

My conscience told me the best thing to do, particularly since I did not have much time before my flight was scheduled to depart, was to take it to lost and found. I weaved through the crowds of people and ended up in front of a security officer. I asked her where I should take the ring, and before she answered me, she questioned where I got it and why I had it.

I explained the situation to her, and she agreed to deliver it to the lost and found herself. She thanked me for returning it, and I headed off to my gate and boarded the airplane.

Although I did not find the owner myself, I did my best to facilitate

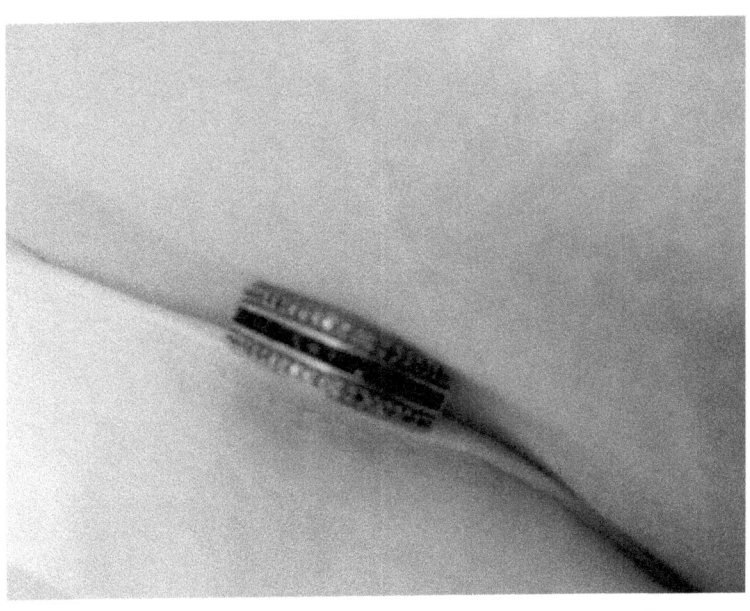

My hope that the ring will be returned to its owner one day

the process. I'm no St. Anthony, but I believe in returning a person's prized possessions if they are found. My mother taught me a very important lesson over and over again. Each time she retold her story about praying to St. Anthony, I remembered how she felt about losing her treasures. She delivered the story with such conviction that anyone who heard it would understand her message. One never knows the significance a single item can hold for another person, regardless of its monetary value. I know the significance of my own pieces, and they are irreplaceable. I can only hope that the ring's owner returned to Midway Airport to find it. If she hasn't yet, the ring will be waiting there when she does.

Chapter Thirteen

Roger, the Crabby Splasher

When I graduated from college, I retained all the theoretical knowledge I could ever hope for. I knew all about algebra, calculus, complicated economic theories, communication, and the intertwining of gender roles in society. I was infected with the no-one-can-stop me complex because, as a member of the millennial generation, I thought any dream I could dream up was entirely possible.

I'd worked hard as a student, and it had paid off in the form of good grades and culminated with my graduation.   I lined up a full-time job with one of the largest companies in the world, and the gig was set to start just a month after I left school.

For all new hires, the company required one of the most extensive training programs I have ever gone through.* On the first week of the job, the company shipped employees off

---

* The training was above and beyond expectations. The company is known in the consumer-packaged goods (CPG) industry for the levels of education that it provides for the people who work for the company. It has been both nationally and globally recognized in business magazines, websites, and other forms of media.

to corporate headquarters, where the bright-eyed and hopeful newbies would roam around aimlessly in massive hordes, a few hundred at each session. The facilitators made sure every moment was action packed. We learned the company history, role-played in mock sales presentations, and accompanied the C-level executives to dinner. When we could squeeze it in around such a hectic schedule, the new recruits and I went out to explore the city and its broad selection of local bars. Since the majority of us were recent college graduates, binge-drinking was part of the norm.

When the week began, I was full of energy, spunk, and inspiration. I couldn't wait to start doing my job and earning money. As the days rolled on, my body became more lethargic. The "real world," as my mother would put it, seemed to be caving in on me. I had to get used to waking up at six a.m. every morning and going to bed at a decent hour. My co-workers felt similar natural reactions as their bodies adjusted to the very grown-up demands, and yawning increased as the week wore on. The restlessness was widespread and noticeable.

Finally, our group made it to Friday. The instructors scheduled us for events until noon, and when we reached the halfway point in the day, we were dismissed and given a boxed lunch to take back with us to the airport. The company provided shuttles to eliminate the expense of individual cab rides, so the group shuffled to the buses and loaded into the seats, meals in hand. An odd silence ensued as everyone gobbled up their sandwiches and chips and completed the meal with a cookie.

I chugged my water to eliminate a hassle during the security checkpoint. I tossed all of my garbage into the trash on the way into the airport and trekked through security. All I could think about was sleeping in my own bed that night. It was time for me to decompress and spend some time with my friends and family. I made it to the gate and waited for the boarding process to begin.

When I sat down in the terminal, it was as if a weight had been lifted off my shoulders. I had successfully completed the first full week of my career, and I could finally focus on rewarding myself with some R&R. It was comforting to know that the only obstacle between me and the commencement of the weekend was an hour-and-a-half flight.

Since we were unable to book our own flights, I was forced to use an airline I did not typically prefer. The boarding process was tedious, causing confusion for many of the passengers. I stood in my place, annoyed with the wait. When I peered out the window to check out the airliner, I realized it was a smaller, regional jet. There really is no difference in these airplanes, but I was not looking forward to squishing and ducking to crawl into a confined space.

Since I am overly observant of my surroundings, I scanned my fellow passengers in the gate area before boarding the plane, and I noticed something quite bizarre. A gentleman, clad in somewhat abnormal clothing, was chatting up a storm with no one. There was no one in the vicinity of the chair where he sat, yet he was carrying on a conversation. Of course all types of people take to the skies, but this was quite odd. My stressful work week did not make his annoying habits any easier to ignore.

The employees finally started calling up segments of people to take their assigned place, and mine was toward the back of the airplane on the left side. I followed my typical routine, locating the row and seat that would be my temporary home, then placing my belongings under the seat in front of me. Just out of curiosity, I looked for the chatty man from the airport and spotted him about fifteen rows ahead of me on the same side, sitting next to a young woman who appeared to be in her late twenties or early thirties. He was still talking out loud to no one.

The flight crew went through the safety spiel, unnecessarily instructing the seasoned travelers how to buckle their seatbelts and prepare for a water landing. The plane moved backward, away from the airport, and we were on our way to Chicago.

I leaned my tired noggin back against the headrest and closed my eyes, hoping to get some decent shut-eye during the short commute so I could recoup a bit for the weekend.

We began taxiing toward the runway as usual, and the flight crew continued to give instructions to the passengers. Having heard it all countless times before, I tuned it all out and morphed it into a quiet hum in my head. I heard the flight attendants sound the buzzer as we approached the runway, and then they announced that we were clear for departure. I expected to hear the familiar sound of the engines booming with airflow to propel us down the runway, but the flight did not go as planned.

Just as the flight attendants began to take their seats for takeoff, the strange man seated some rows ahead of mine turned on his call button. Any frequent flier knows that once the captain indicates that the flight is cleared for takeoff, everyone must remained seated – passengers and flight attendants included – until a safe altitude is reached. We were not yet off the ground, so the flight attendant scooted over to him to find out what he needed.

I watched and rolled my eyes with annoyance. The flight attendant's face was alarmed at whatever the man had told her, and she gave some sort of signal to her fellow A+ Airlines employee near the front of the cabin, who then promptly phoned the captain. A few dings sounded one right after another, and the ladies scurried around the galley, collecting glasses, ice, and an abundance of water, which I assumed was for the odd duck up in front of me.

Moments later, the attendants ran back over to his row and handed him the glasses of water and some salty crackers. By then, all the passengers were fully engaged in watching the spectacle. We began to chat amongst ourselves, asking if anyone knew what was going on. We came to the conclusion that the man was suffering from some medical emergency, possibly a heart attack.

I watched as the flight attendants continued to hand glasses of water to the man. Instead of drinking the fluid, he dumped the entire glass over the top of his head and all over the young woman seated next to him. Though it might sound insensitive, my initial reaction was a small burst of laughter. *Did*

I just see a grown man dump a glass of water all over another passenger and himself?

As the freak show continued, the pilot thrust the airplane forward down the runway at top speed. My confusion was furthered because I could not believe we were taking off with such antics and possibly a medical emergency in progress. At that moment, an announcement came over the loudspeaker to inform us that there was, in fact, a medical emergency onboard requiring immediate attention, and we were told we would be taxiing back to the nearest gate.

I had to wonder what was wrong with the strange man who'd been talking to himself. It was the first time I'd ever encountered a serious problem on a plane. Normally, the biggest dilemma is a delay in drinks and peanuts being served. I'd read about medical emergencies occurring during flights, but I had never experienced one before.

Being approximately fifteen rows behind all the action, my view was limited. None of us toward the back of the aircraft could tell if it was a life-or-death situation. I grew increasingly uncomfortable as I pondered whether or not the man was in real danger.

The captain floored it, so to speak, and sped back to the terminal, and within about thirty-five seconds, we arrived at the gate.

When we pulled up, fire trucks, two ambulances, and medical personnel swarmed the plane. The flight attendants instructed everyone to remain seated to allow the medical team to access the gentleman in the confined space. He was still nonsensically chatting up a storm, but I couldn't quite comprehend what he was saying.

As soon as the door to the aircraft swung open, rescuers rushed in. The emergency crew bombarded the man with questions and swept him off the aircraft within a few minutes.

I later found out that it's nearly impossible to perform any sort of medical care on someone in the small confines of such a plane. He was taken just inside the tunnel all of us had walked down just minutes earlier to board the plane.

The captain and flight attendants made a few more announcements, apologizing for the inconvenience. They informed everyone that the flight would be delayed until the passenger who'd been removed was released by the paramedics and pronounced stable enough to fly. In the meantime, we were given permission to get up, use the restroom, and access our bags in the overhead compartments.

The cabin filled with people's voices as everyone speculated, and those who'd been near him stated that he'd been telling everyone that he was "hot." When the captain indicated that the flight was going to take off, he was worried that he would not be able to cool down quickly enough to be comfortable. Instead of asking the flight crew to turn the temperature down, he lied and claimed he was suffering from a much more severe medical problem.

The flight attendants realized he seemed to be having trouble breathing. His face was flushed and patchy red, and he was sweating profusely. Following protocol, they had to assume he was in cardiac arrest. When they brought over the only resources they had to try and comfort him, he chose to pour the water all over himself to cool down, soaking the poor woman seated next to him. A group of passengers had surrounded her and were trying to help her dry off. Flight attendants brought her paper towels, though those did little to alleviate the sopping-wet clothing she wore.

When the passengers found out it was a crying-wolf faux disaster, they snickered at the man. He had selfishly delayed an entire plane full of people and caused a major scene simply because he felt a bit warm and uncomfortable. When it comes to those who have medical issues, I am quite sympathetic, but the idea of this man faking a heart attack to cool himself down was unfathomable to me. I overheard other passengers asking flight attendants how to proceed once we arrived in Chicago. Because of the delay, they would miss their connecting flights that were to take them to their final destinations. The airline employees instructed them to contact one of the agents at the podium as soon as they reached the city, and they could be rebooked on a different flight.

We sat at the gate for a long hour and forty minutes extra because of that man. As soon as the medical team released him, he reentered the plane. I don't know if I would have been brave enough to resurface after pulling a stunt like that, but he didn't seem to have any trouble walking up the aisle and taking his seat, as if nothing had happened.

The flight attendants were forced to go over the safety procedures and announcements again, and finally the captain made it to the runway without a hitch. The flight took off and was relatively normal after all that commotion.

When the plane touched down in Chicago, I was ecstatic. After such a grueling week and an additional SNAFU in transportation, I was on the ground in my hometown, and I couldn't have been happier. I could have almost kissed the pavement, but I abstained, as it would have been a bit cliché and ridiculous looking.

That man's behavior should not have surprised me that day. He disregarded his surroundings, and the focus was solely on him. Ultimately, it was a blatant realization for me that the world is a massive place full of so many different kinds of people. I was no longer under my parents' roof, and the sheltering bubble of college life was quickly crumbling around me. That experience was a wake-up call for me.

I'd started on that Monday with more confidence in myself and my abilities than any one person should have. I was a rock star as a student. I'd earned exceptional grades without putting forth the exorbitant effort that some of my peers had to, since academics have always come relatively easy for me. I had no reason to believe that my full-time career or any of the baggage that went along with it would be any different, but that flight showed me how wrong I was.

People adapt to their surroundings. Because of that, one of my first scares on a flight, I learned to take each person and day with a grain of salt. The company would have been proud to know that even the flight home was challenging; it was a foreshadowing of just how complicated work and life can get sometimes when we least expect it.

I dealt with some of the most bullheaded and stubborn people during my tenure at that company. The clients I serviced made my day-to-day job difficult. They fought with me, disagreed with the decisions I made, and argued about how we should work together in the future. My new existence in the working world was much different from the comfortable, naïve place I'd been living in for the past four years. In the end, that flight was just a prelude to what I was going to experience when I was immersed in the general public, and I suppose A+ Airlines was as good a place as any for me to have that learning experience.

Chapter Fourteen

John, the Paternal Soldier

In my spare time, what little I actually have, I volunteer regularly to recruit prospective MBA students for my alma mater, Indiana University. Each spring and fall, the school hosts recruitment events for the Kelley Direct program, which I graduated from in May 2011. The school administration believes that one of the best ways to sell the school to potential students is to include alumni in the mix.

Individuals who are exploring their higher education options have tens of thousands of schools to choose from, and if they are to choose to study at the Kelley School of Business, there must be a compelling reason. My sole purpose for being involved in those meetings was to serve, basically, as an IU cheerleader[*] and sell the attendees on the best academic program I have ever

---

[*]   The term "cheerleader" in this context is meant to imply my enthusiasm and promotion for the program. It most definitely does not include any sort of short skirt. I was never cut out to have that much pep. I did have a friend at IU who cheered during every game for the school, and I commend her for the exuberant energy she applied to her duty.

participated in. I am passionate about IU, so I found this to be an easy and enjoyable task.

During the fall of 2011, I jumped at the opportunity to join some of my fellow classmates at a recruiting event, and I accepted the e-mailed invite within seconds. It was the first session I would attend as an alumnus, and I was excited about the opportunity. The invitation indicated that the event would begin on Friday afternoon and conclude during a formal dinner Saturday night. Volunteers were instructed to book hotel rooms for both evenings, as well as flights to travel into the area.

The tentative agenda that outlined exact times, places, and activities for the two-day event. Three of my former classmates and I were scheduled to speak on a panel, answering any and all questions regarding the program. Since I love to boast about the outstanding program, it was right up my alley. I rummaged through the message, quickly skipping over the less important details, and without even thinking about it, I opened a window on my computer to head to A+ Airlines website so I could arrange for my flight.

At the time, I'd just begun my sales position at a pivotal point, when the main marketing contact at our company decided to leave. My boss had asked if I would help out with the responsibilities of that position, as well as continue the job duties of my assigned title. The double-duty would only be a temporary solution while we interviewed candidates to find a replacement for the marketing coordinator. I assumed those additional tasks without hesitation, happy to help and eager to make a good impression. Little did I realize just how much additional work it would entail.

I was responsible for leading meetings, delegating tasks to others, and managing the packaging labels for our customers – all in addition to my regular duties as a salesperson. Luckily, a knowledgeable team of support personnel helped me get the hang of things quickly. I worked diligently to make sure the job was executed with utmost quality and timeliness, but that made leaving at a reasonable time on Friday afternoons quite difficult.

The only way I would make it to IU in time for the majority of the festivities was to hop on a forty-five-minute flight from Chicago to Indianapolis.

I perused the available flights, and it seemed wasteful to spend such a frivolous amount of money for air travel when I could have easily driven. Still, considering my duties at work, I could not bear to drive the three-and-a-half hour commute after such a long day, so I found a time that coincided with the end of my day and booked it. I couldn't wait for to take part, and I knew it was going to be a memorable experience on the campus I loved.

Time flew by for the next few weeks, and the weekend of the event was soon approaching. I bragged to all of my IU alumni friends about how much fun I was going to have on campus; they yelled and cooed at me with envy. I packed my bags with cream-and-crimson items and loaded them into the car.

The work day zoomed by quickly as I ran around tying up all the loose ends before the weekend. When the clock struck four thirty, it was time for my mad dash to the airport to catch my jet over to Indianapolis. The drive, parking, and security check-in were a blur, my mind focused entirely on the impending weekend activities. I couldn't wait to be back in my old stomping grounds, and I felt nostalgic just thinking about it.

I boarded the plane and found my assigned seat. The person booked to sit next to me had not arrived yet, so I took the opportunity to organize my belongings organized. I placed my carryon luggage under the seat in front of me and found a book to read, intending to catch up on a story I'd been procrastinating to finish for quite some time. It seemed like a perfect time to enjoy a little rest and relaxation in preparation for my exciting weekend. I never got the chance to dive into the book on that flight, but I most certainly did walk away with a story.

Almost as soon as I removed the book from my baggage, a gentleman dressed in military clothing sat down next to me. I lifted my head up for a glimpse of who it was, and he simultaneously greeted me with a warm, gentile smile. He introduced himself as "John" and shook my hand with a firm grip. I smiled back and told him my name, the typical greeting for two strangers.

John appeared to be in his mid-forties. He had dark brown hair and stood at least six feet tall, though it was difficult to tell since I was already sitting. He was dressed in dark, greenish-tan camouflage and what my dad would have referred to as "work boots."* His hair was styled in a buzz cut, and his face was clean shaven.

John exuded a light about him, almost an aura. He smiled at many of the passengers who entered the aircraft and passed him in the aisle. Some stared back with nothing but blank looks on their faces. Others nodded or smirked. His unique warmth toward strangers had the same impact on others as it did on me. I had never met someone so cordial, happy, and bubbly, and his nature was calming in a way. He sat upright in his chair with the utmost confidence about him, though he wasn't the slightest bit arrogant. His demeanor not only piqued my interest, but it also relieved me somehow.

When the passengers were all settled into their seats, John turned toward me and began asking questions, starting with what I did for a living. I was honored that someone serving the greatest and most powerful military force in the world cared about the meager impact I might have on the economy. I offered him my thirty-second elevator speech, letting him know I was a salesperson for toaster pastries and granola bars and that my job was to travel around the country and meet with clients to sell them on new concepts, products, and opportunities in their unique markets. It was such a redundant speech that I could have played it on a tape recorder if I'd had one around my neck.

Similar to most people, his eyes perked up when he

---

* I call these "work boots" because that is the name I grew up using. I took the liberty to look up the official name, however, and John was wearing modern combat boots, a light tan color with a dull surface and yellowish laces that go all the way up the front panel. They rise about halfway up a man's calf to protect the lower half of the leg.

heard that I sold delicious treats for a living. Although his body language mimicked the general population, there was a comical spin to John's dialect when he asked if I had any samples he could approve. He definitely had a sense of humor, but unfortunately, I had no samples to offer him. I did take the opportunity to inform him of all the local grocery stores where he could find the tasty treats, and he nodded and promised to try them when he returned home.

I continued our conversation by asking a silly question about what he did for a living, since his attire was a clear indication of his occupation. He joked, "Um, as if you can't tell, I'm in the Army."

I chuckled a little at his dry, but charming humor, which I found delightful.

His next explanation was a conglomerate of information regarding his actual military responsibilities. Unfamiliar with the technical terms and jargon,** I sat in my seat and nodded mindlessly at his foreign-sounding descriptions. He mentioned countries such as Afghanistan, which immediately triggered the thought of danger in my head. My only source of information about such things has been the media and the news. Therefore, anything pertaining to struggles, missions, or the Middle East in general worries me, particularly for the safety and wellbeing of the soldiers stationed there.

I allowed John to continue, and he informed me of some of his recent explorations around the world. I could only chime in to show him I was listening, even though my comprehension was somewhat scattered.

John was patient with my elementary questions, and

** My unfamiliarity with the military lingo and references should have been blatantly obvious with my referral of "work boots" in describing John's shoes. As with any group or sector in the community, the language and words used to describe positions, responsibilities, and duties is much different than the verbiage I use. I experience the same phenomenon when I attempt to discuss my fiancé's occupation of metallurgical engineering.

I made my best effort to be conservative and overly broad in what I asked. I wanted to appear interested without being too invasive of his privacy. Even with some of my closest friends and family, I've always been hesitant to really dive into the depths of information that is ingrained in anyone that has served our country. I fear blurting out an offensive or obtrusive question.

As John continued to babble on a bit more, I asked him some more personal questions. I inquired about his wife, children, family, and friends, and his answer was something I couldn't fully comprehend.

John had been deployed for the past year, and he had not seen his two children or wife in person during that entire time. His communication with them had been limited to a few sessions per week, mostly via telephone or Skype. He would see them for the first time in twelve grueling months as soon as he stepped off that airplane.

I think my mouth dropped open for ten seconds straight. I talk to my parents, fiancé, sister, and friends at least a few times per week, often much more. I look to the people who are closest to me to confirm that each deciding detail is the right one. Their support is what enables me to be confident about my choices. For the past year, John's life had been dictated by his obligations to the military. He did not even have the opportunity to hug or kiss his children and could only communicate with them briefly via telephone, all while his life was on the line each and every day.

My family and friends all reside within a short driving distances from my house. At that moment, as John spoke about his trials and tribulations of the past twelve months, I realized how lucky I am. I have the choice to see the people I care about anytime, a privilege I often take for granted. His interaction was greatly limited to the available resources provided for him within the confines of war and military service, and it certainly didn't seem like much. It was difficult for me to fathom it. I then knew why he was glowing and so happy and kind to all around him. He was overflowing with happiness because he was going to see his family – finally.

That short, puddle-jumper flight was the second leg of his trip home. Since Chicago's O'Hare Airport is a major hub for so many cities throughout the country, he flew into Chicago for the initial segment of his flight. John had only slept a few hours the night before on the plane ride back into the United States, and he'd been anticipating the next thirty minutes for the last year. It was truly incredible to think about.

John talked much about his beloved children, starting with his son, a seven-year-old and the quintessential boy. He loved fishing, baseball, playing outside with his friends, and spending time with his grandpa. Since John had been gone on military assignments for certain parts of his son's childhood, his father had taken the initiative to involve himself in the boy's life, making sure there was always a reliable father figure present. He taught his grandson how to play sports and about the strategy behind each game. John revealed that his father was the person he looked up to the most, a perfect role model for his young boy. John's father taught all the important life lessons to his grandson that he had once taught to John. As John told me about this, he smiled, and his eyes became a little misty.

John missed out his son's summer Little League games, but he always received updates via e-mail from his wife. According to John, his son was "quite the first baseman," and the soldier beamed with justifiable pride as he talked about it. He laughed when he told me about his wife screaming and yelling on the sidelines. She didn't care what anyone else thought as long as her son knew he had her support, and she was his biggest fan.

John was looking forward to returning to his family in the fall, at the start of football season. He reminisced about three generations of men in his family watching football on Sunday afternoons, their coveted guy time. His father would bring over some beer, and he would heat up some frozen pizzas for the three of them to munch on as they called play-by-play commentary from their sofa and chairs. The room would explode in an uproar of cheers when their team scored touchdowns, and loud boos would ensue when the referees called an unfair penalty against them. It was easy to see that John longed to return to that Sunday tradition.

Next, he described his daughter, a twelve-year-old who was convinced her parents were wrong about everything, as most pre-teens are. I knew exactly what he was talking about. She always wanted to make plans with her friends and have sleepovers at their houses, and John said family functions seemed to "annoy" her. I smiled and remembered when I was at that stage of my life, something we all go through, and I chuckled and nodded my head in understanding. I assured the worried father that it was only a phase and that his daughter would eventually come back around.

John regretted the lack of discipline while he was out of the country. He considered much of it to be rebellion because her father was not in the home enough. I reassured John that most pre-teens go through stages of love and hate for their parents, a fluid cycle. I informed him that he should prepare to endure it until she hit nineteen or twenty, and he rolled his eyes and laughed at me simultaneously. John made sure to mention more than once that he loved his daughter and that he hoped things would turn around with her, and I promised him they eventually would. After all, I've been a twelve-year-old girl before.

As I sat on our flight listening to the man describe his family, I began to feel as if I knew them. He painted such a vivid description of his loved ones and added to his verbal depiction by taking out a small photograph of his kids, taken a few years prior. The edges were ripped slightly, and the color had faded, but I could still see the two beautiful children he'd boasted about. The well-worn condition of the photo led me to believe he'd taken it with him on most of his world travels and military adventures, and I was sure it had comforted him on many lonely and homesick nights.

While I drifted off in my own thoughts, he segued into a story about how he'd met his wife "Carry." John had known her since their childhood, as his parents were best friends with another couple who just so happened to have a daughter John's age. John chased her around as a kid and admitted that he had an elementary crush on her. He knew at an early age that she was his dream woman, and he teased that she "loved the pursuit," and that he wasn't about to give up on her because he knew all along that she was the one.

Throughout high school and college, Carry dated many boyfriends. John described them all as "losers" who were unworthy of her time. His blunt attitude made me smile, and it was clear how much he cared for her, even back then. From the way John described her, it seemed no one would have been good enough for her. He said he was to go out with her and was willing to wait until she was single. When the opportunity came, John jumped at his chance to ask her out.

He anticipated a positive response from her, but that wasn't what he got, and she rejected him at least a few times. Finally, he went to her mother and asked her to talk to Carry about going on one date with him. Her mother was impressed that he would go to such lengths and agreed to mention the idea to Carry but said she would not put pressure on her daughter. Somehow, her mother's suggestion worked. He never did find out what Carry's mom bribed her with, but she was able to sway her daughter's opinion.

John planned what he thought would be a perfect date, but much to his dismay and to Carry's, nothing went as planned. He showed up late to pick her up, was stopped by a police officer for speeding, and ended up taking her home early at her request. He couldn't believe how bad it had gone and said it was one of the only times he'd actually embarrassed himself on a first date.

I nodded my head to show my empathy. I didn't want to make him feel worse, but it sounded like a huge disaster.

But then, the best thing in the world happened to John when Carry called him back a few days later and asked for a do-over. John couldn't believe his good fortune. The girl of his dreams was now chasing him.

I thought he was over-thinking her request, but I didn't tell him that. Instead, I wanted him to bask in the glory of his romantic story.

He abruptly ended the story of the dating game by saying, "And the rest was history." He was thrilled to report that they'd been married for fifteen glorious years.

I congratulated him on the longevity of their nuptials, and I had to appreciate the happiness he exuded when he spoke about his family.

As John bantered on about his family, I lost track of time on the airplane. When I took a brief hiatus from his life history, I noticed that we were descending. The short flight seemed like only a few minutes because I was so preoccupied with the man who was pouring his heart out next to me. The flight attendants were milling about the cabin collecting plastic cups and snack wrappers, and John and I both tidied our row up to prepare for the landing.

The jet touched down, and the flight attendant made the usual announcement. While we were taxiing on the runway, no one was allowed to remove their seatbelt or get up. Luggage in the overhead bins might have shifted during the flight, so we were all warned to be careful when removing it on our way out. We were thanked for flying on A+ Airlines. Since I fly so frequently, I muted the recording; I'd heard it so many times that I could have recited it from memory if one of the flight attendants had been plagued with laryngitis.

The instructions that day were no different, until the end of the spiel, when the flight attendant unexpectedly asked everyone on the plane to give a round of applause to thank the military personnel on the plane. John's military attire stood out from a mile away amongst a horde of civilians in street clothes, so it was clear that she was talking about him. She also requested that he be allowed to exit the plane first.

The passengers initiated a boisterous round of applause with a few coos and howls mixed in. While I clapped my own hands, I glanced over at a blushing soldier. John just sat there for a moment with a stern, humble face, grinning and glad to be home. In that moment of pure appreciation and thankfulness from a group of Americans, a chill shivered its way down my spine and channeled throughout my entire body. Truly, it was a special moment for John – and for all of us who were lucky enough to be in his presence moments before his glorious and much-deserved reunion with his family.

John thanked me for the conversation, even though he'd done most of the talking. I let him know that it was nice to meet him and wished him the best of luck in the future with his family and the armed forces. I was glad to take that moment to thank him for the selfless services he had contributed to the country.

The plane came to a final halt at the gate, and the overhead seatbelt indicator buzzed to indicate it was safe to remove the belt. John unbuckled his and retrieved his carryon luggage from under his seat. He headed toward the front of the plane as instructed.

I saw John exit the plane, leading the rest of the passengers, who were eager to get out of the aircraft and be on their way to their final destinations. I grabbed my luggage out of the overhead compartment and scurried toward the front of the plane.

I don't typically check my luggage into the cargo part of the airplane,* as this allows me to quickly exit the airport and beat the crowds. The physical layout of that particular airport forced me to walk past the luggage corrals to reach the rental car desks. Normally, I would have been annoyed to have to take the scenic route, but on this occasion, I was glad to, as it afforded me a rare opportunity to witness a very special moment.

As I turned the corner from the massive hall of gates toward the security checkpoint, I noticed some commotion and a gathering of people. There were multicolored balloons, a white banner, and some sort of celebratory outbursts taking place. I was

---

* On my way home from Iceland one year, my bags were lost for a few days. The fear of my personal belongings never finding their way back to me was so overwhelming that I stopped checking luggage under the plane. Despite the annoyance and inconvenience, I choose to bang and bash my luggage through the terminals and plop them into the overhead bins in the aircraft, so I'll know where it is at all times.

too far away to really grasp what was going on, but as I neared the narrow gateway, I was able to read the banner: "Welcome Home, Dad!"

Instantaneously, chills ran up my spine. It was a homecoming celebration for John, and I walked right past the people I'd just heard so much about – the folks who made John's life worth living. I had the greatest respect for his reunion and didn't want to make myself noticeable, for those are the moments in life that will never be re-created to full effect, and they shouldn't be ruined by intruders.

I couldn't help but stare at the group of people surrounding my row mate. I recognized the boots from a few feet away, but I couldn't see John for all of the fanfare. His face was buried in a woman's shoulder, presumably Carry's. His daughter and son were intertwined between their parents with blank stares of awe on their faces. The fluorescent lighting sparkled off their faces, highlighting the trickles of tears that streamed down their cheeks. I heard faint murmurs of sobbing noises and the sniffle of noses. Some elderly people, whom I determined to be John's and Carry's parents, were smiling from ear to ear, saltwater rivers adorning their cheeks.

As I witnessed that sincere, genuine reconnection of a family, my eyes began to well up with tears. For me, it wasn't really about the emotions and hardship endured by John and his family. I was thinking of all of the people I care about. I couldn't imagine living without them for a year as John had. His family had been torn apart by duty, only connected by social media and limited telephone conversations. I, on the other hand, have the opportunity to chat with and see my friends and family at my own free will. Oddly, the reason I can enjoy such freedoms is because of men like John. I was affected by his service, knowing that he and his family had given up their luxuries to help provide for mine and for so many others – something I'll be forever grateful for.

I never had the chance to thank John, and I wished I would have. When I mill through the airport now, I pay more attention to the young men and women in military garb. Each time I see one of them, I think about John and his love for his family. I'd started out that weekend thinking of my too-long journey from Chicago to Indianapolis to attend a recruiting event for my school. Little did I know that the man sitting next to me was at the end of a yearlong journey on which there was so much more at stake. I was honored to have had the opportunity to converse with him briefly during our ride.

I believe the invite to that recruiting session meant more than just what was on the surface. I learned a massive lesson about humanity and life on that short trip. I revisited my feelings toward my family and realized just how valuable my time with them is. I could never ask for a more supportive set of people in my life. This major lesson reminded me of just how valuable people are. In that way, Indiana University taught me one last lesson, even if it wasn't through a textbook and didn't cost me a cent of tuition.

Chapter Fifteen

Cathy, the Chatty Civilian

As most of you realize, September 11, 2001 resulted in many changes in the airline industry and the associated regulations. Federal laws were passed for more stringent security measures. Those who have migrated through security barricades, U.S. customs, or the mile-long lines in the airport understand the changes firsthand. Because of the terrorist attacks of 9/11, the Federal Aviation Administration (FAA) is now like a protective big brother, and the agency strives to keep air travel for all passengers safe.

In order to comply with the established regulations, airlines have changed their requirements both on the ground and in flight, and the processes and protocols have been reinvented. Flight attendants have more power and authority over the passengers that venture onto their planes. Unfortunately, not everyone feels it is vital to comply wholeheartedly with all of the rules in order to ensure safety for all passengers. There have been numerous accounts of individuals disregarding the instructions.

Those who fly often realize that the pre-flight procedures are relatively routine. It becomes a natural part of traveling, almost automatic. As I've mentioned, I often don't even pay attention to the loudspeaker announcements because I can practically recite them by heart. I could probably reenact each ding of the buzzer, pre- and post-boarding, announcement and the entire safety spiel on how to properly inflate the yellow floatation life vest.

The flight attendants are required by law to repeat the mundane speech each time, and it's easy to pick out the less-than-frequent fliers because of the worried look on their faces at the sound of "emergency water landing" escaping the mouths of the flight attendant.

One of my favorite co-workers and I use stories as a temporary escape from the mundane administrative duties in our office. During a slow afternoon, I ventured over to his cubicle and sat down in his guest chair. He immediately started talking business, and we discussed some of the normal topics about our shared employer, but nothing new surfaced.

When I realized that shop talk was a moot point on that lackluster afternoon, I was quick to avert the conversation to a more leisurely topic. The man told some of the funniest stories I'd ever heard, and he was a natural at it. He was something like Morgan Freeman, capable of using his narration-suited voice to suggest suspense, love, or mystery at just the perfect moments, capturing the audience with his perfect tone. He also incorporated a myriad of hand gestures and arm movements to emphasize when necessary, and his stories often had me laughing so hard that my sides hurt.

In desperate need of a break from the monotony of Excel spreadsheets, I begged him to dig deep in his collection and pull out a good one.

He agreed and took a few seconds to think through his arsenal of personal anecdotes. All of a sudden, he perked up and admitted that he'd thought of a good one, promising that I'd never believe it. I had a feeling it was going to be interesting, and I was correct.

During that particular week, the anniversary of September 11 was a fresh story in the news. I only assumed that it was part

190

of his inspiration for the memory he chose to share. He began the story by indicating that he was venturing out on a trip for work. Being a frequent traveler as well, he was accustomed to the same predictable flight processes. Hundreds of passengers were herded through security, hustled to the gate, and boarded onto the airplane like cattle. It was the same routine over and over again.

Amused by the human condition, my colleague always preferred the back of the airplane so he could people-watch as the other passengers made their way to their seats. He placed his belongings under the seat in front of him and checked out the people sitting within his proximity. Usually, he would sit there quietly and mind his own business, but this day was an exception to the rule, as he couldn't help but eavesdrop on a conversation between one of the flight attendants and a passenger sitting within earshot.

The FAA requires all airlines to comply with a standard set of rules and regulations.* There are specific procedures that are followed each and every flight, without variation. Part of the protocol for leaving the gate involves an official "forward and aft preparation of doors," accompanied by an announcement that the task has been completed.

After the doors are locked securely, flight attendants are required to make an announcement to instruct passengers to turn off all electronic devices. Since technology has exploded into a virtual necessity, hundreds of individual devices have to be powered down before takeoff on every flight. This results in a choir of beeps and chimes from cell phones, iPods, MP3 players, e-readers, iPads, and any other portable electronic gadget as they all shut down. The rule applies to every passenger onboard, but unfortunately, during my co-worker's flight, one woman felt as

---

* The government and FAA really couldn't make it any easier for passengers, airlines, officials, employees, and anyone else with access to the Internet to read and understand their rules. They are published officially on the website for the public at: http://www.faa. gov/regulations_policies/faa_regulations/.

though she was the exception.

"Chatty Cathy," as my co-worker referred to her, continued to talk on her cell phone for a good three to four minutes after the announcement came over the intercom. There were over a hundred passengers onboard, so it took the staff a few minutes to notice her disobedience. They continued the safety speech, walking up and down the aisles to make sure all seatbelts were fastened securely.

When one flight attendant approached Cathy and instructed her a second time to turn her cell phone off, the reaction was not pleasant. Cathy retorted, "If you'd stop talking and leave me alone, I'll be able to finish my conversation." Her tone implied that the flight attendant's request was a major inconvenience, and Cathy was appalled that she would have to cut her conversation short.

My co-worker's eyes bulged as big as saucers when he witnessed the woman's snarky reaction. As a passenger, Cathy was required to follow the directions given by the flight attendants, and her rude, sarcastic rebuttal to a simple request was outlandish.

The flight attendant retorted by telling her in a stern voice that it was imperative that the device be shut down immediately. Cathy ignored the direction and continued to chat on the phone. As my co-worker was telling me the intricate details, I sat there with my mouth wide open and my right hand cupped over it. Not only was her reaction rude, but it was also illegal. I could not even fathom someone being so self-centered and having such a poor attitude when asked to do something so simple for the safety of everyone onboard.

All the nearby passengers stared at her in disbelief, as one would look at a student who'd just sassed the teacher. She blatantly disregarded every instruction that was given to her over and over again. The man she was flying with, whom my co-worker assumed to be her husband, made a halfhearted attempt to prompt her to turn off the phone, but she would not even listen to him. At that juncture, he threw his arms up to signal that his weak attempt was a futile effort and that the woman was not going to listen to anyone and would do as she well pleased – or the overgrown brat thought.

Finally, when she heard the engines beginning to roar with force, she completed her conversation and hung up the phone. My co-worker thought the flight would continue to the runway as planned, but he noticed something different. The pilot began making a circle to turn back toward the terminal. Almost simultaneously, his voice blasted over the speaker system: "Apparently, someone onboard does not wish to fly with us today. We will drop the unrelenting passenger off at the gate before we head to our destination, ladies and gentlemen."

After the announcement, all the passengers began to clap uncontrollably, cheering on the pilot's decision to remove the insolent woman from the aircraft. My co-worker compared the noise to a Major League Baseball game, complete with howls and cat-calls and cheering while the plane headed back toward the origination gate.

Cathy rolled her eyes in disgust; the support from the other passengers clearly offended her. My co-worker said she was cussing and spewing snide remarks at the onboard crew, as if it were their fault. She was not about to take the blame for her actions, and her presumed-to-be husband was wearing a hybrid look of nausea and regret.

Almost instantaneously, a surplus of uniformed officials swarmed the aircraft and marched toward Cathy. The flight attendants surrounded her to prevent her from trying to escape. Passengers pointed in the culprit's direction to indicate to the police who was causing the ruckus.

As the police approached, Cathy began to outwardly deny that she'd done anything wrong. She ranted about her rights, demanding that justice be served, sounding quite rehearsed and as if it was not her first encounter with the law. The police began the process of reciting the Miranda rights to her, then put her hands behind her back and zip-tied them together for makeshift handcuffs. They then forced her to walk toward the exit near the cockpit, as if she were a common criminal, which I guess she was at that point. The police asked her significant other to follow them back through the terminal.

My co-worker and the other remaining passengers stared at her as she was escorted off the plane. She was shouting, demanding a refund, and claiming that A+ Airlines was the worst airline she had ever flown on simply because they'd attempted to make her follow the rules. By this time, her voice had morphed into something that was more like a screech because she was yelling at such a high decibel, an unjustified reaction by anyone who felt guilty about their disruptive behavior. Cathy's behavior was something one might expect to see in a movie, when characters act flamboyant and exaggerate to get a point across.

The crew apologized for Cathy's antics after she was removed from the airplane, but the passengers did not blame them and were happy the woman had been removed, murmuring their glee that she'd gotten what she deserved. My co-worker shrugged to the person sitting next to him and laughed a bit.

Once the crew was reorganized, they announced the departure of the aircraft again. Because they hadn't yet taken off, thanks to Chatty Cathy, they had to go over the safety instructions again. This time, each and every person onboard obeyed. My co-worker finished the story by telling me that the rest of the flight went as planned. As he reminisced about his experience, he laughed at it in disgust.

I sat in the chair with my mouth open, shaking my head in disbelief. I could not believe anyone would have the audacity to disregard the rules in such a blatant way. Anyone who has flown post 9/11 knows how serious these rules are taken by all employees and passengers. The government enacted these regulations for safety. They are simple enough to understand and obey, and any passenger who purchases a ticket to fly is, in essence, agreeing to abide by them.

The airline industry has cycled through some drastic changes in recent history. The process of getting on an airplane to travel from a hub to a destination has many more steps than it used to. Instead of moseying through some basic security checks, passengers are thoroughly searched, prodded, and questioned to ensure everyone's safe travel, all for the wellbeing of everyone onboard.

As in any situation, there will always be that one person who chooses to disrupt, disobey, and cause total mayhem because they feel they are above the law. The negative attention Cathy drew toward herself that day was irreparable to her reputation, but she did teach everyone a lesson. She was the perfect example out of how not to act on an airplane.

This story was a great reminder that one's reputation is built on their past. It is irrevocable and unchangeable, so it is crucial that we are cognizant of our actions each and every day. We never know who is watching, listening, or mimicking our behavior. A person's reputation is the one thing that remains with them forever, even after they are gone. For me, this lesson was short and sweet, but very impactful.

Chapter Sixteen

Jack, the Heart Throb

I have always gone to my mom for advice, as I know she'll always shoot it to me straight. She refuses to sugarcoat her answers or tell me just what she thinks I want to hear just because I am her daughter. Instead, she gives her honest opinion, even if it's not the easiest thing to say. She is willing to vocalize her disapproval for anything that doesn't feel right, and as an adult, I've learned to appreciate her brutal honesty. I've also come to realize that she has been right on more occasions than I can count.

When I asked for her guidance as a kid, she often told me, "Listen to your gut." At the time, I didn't quite understand what she meant, and I even wondered if she was referring to the literal rumbling and gurgling noises it made when I was hungry. I knew it had to be good advice because it came from her, but it took some time to grasp the metaphorical meaning behind her message.

I gained a slight understanding of this when I made a very bad choice in high school. One of my best friends called me up on a Saturday night to ask if I wanted to go out with her, and of course I jumped at the chance. We planned for her to come and pick me up, and we would go have dinner together. I ran to my bedroom to change clothes, and just as I did, the phone rang again. This time, it was a guy in whom I was quite interested, calling to ask me to a movie. I hesitated a little while I thought about my prior commitment, but ultimately, the girlfriend lost to the guy.

I scurried into my mom's bedroom to ask what I should tell my friend to get out of our plans without hurting her feelings too much. Being a teenager who was just starting to grow fond of the opposite sex, I couldn't pass up the opportunity to go out with a guy I'd had my eye on, though looking back on it now, it was not one of the proudest moments of my life. Sadly, I wasn't yet aware of the fact that one's reputation sticks with them forever.

When I gave my mom the spiel for the night's plans, she shook her head back and forth and told me I should stick with the original plan to hang out with my girlfriend. She thought it was unfair of me to ditch my plans just because someone else called after the fact.

I should have listened to her, but at the time, I was sure she was old-fashioned and didn't know what she was talking about and was just trying to ruin my fun. I told her I was going to cancel my plans with my friend anyway and go catch a flick with Boy Wonder.

When I made the phone call to my friend, I discovered what it meant to listen to one's gut. As soon as she got on the phone, I instantaneously spat out a lie and told her I did not feel well and I'd decided to stay in for the night.

As the fib exited my mouth, it was as if a massive boulder sank down into the depths of my stomach. A streak of weakness spread throughout my nervous system, and my gut literally ached with the weight of the lie, my body's involuntary message that what I was doing was wrong.

Being the good friend she was, the rejected one called my parents later in the evening to see if I was feeling better. My mother would not lie to cover for my indiscretions and told her

I'd gone out with someone else that night. Because of my poor decision, my friend didn't talk to me for the next four months. I should have listened to my gut.

From that point on, I knew it was best to listen to what my instincts tell me. Since then, my stomach has often warned me out of doing the wrong thing. It's unpredictable and unprecedented, but I know that when it happens, it is a sign to be a little more aware. It is always a tell-tale sign that something is not exactly right. I'm not sure how it works, but usually the feeling is right on target.

One fall morning, I was on my way to the airport for a business trip. Something in my gut told me something wasn't right, so I assumed I'd just forgotten something I needed for my trip.

I began shuffling through my packed bags, certain that something important had been left out. I found everything I needed, and it didn't seem that anything had been left behind, so I was baffled as to what was causing the uneasiness in my very core. I shrugged it off as I hopped on the shuttle bus from the airport parking lot to the terminal.

As I moseyed through the airport to the security gates, I continued to sweep over my luggage for something that might be missing. Nothing surfaced or stuck out drastically, so I chalked it up to simple paranoia. I arrived at my flight with plenty of time to spare and chose to spend the extra minutes charging my computer so I could get some work done during the two-hour flight, as it would be the perfect time to catch up.

Before I knew it, the standard routine began, and the herds of passengers were called to board the plane. I was so used to the process that it was second nature to me. I found an aisle seat near the middle of the plane and sat down. Within thirty minutes, everyone had boarded, the pre-flight procedures had been done, and the plane was airborne.

As soon as the announcement for approved portable electronics sounded over the intercom, I pulled my laptop out, hoping that concentrating on my work might dismiss the uneasy feeling that lingered. Unfortunately, I was wrong.

About forty minutes into the flight, I noticed people gathering at the front of the airplane. Since there are strict regulations against that, it caught my attention. The flight attendants seemed to be shouting orders to everyone, and I noticed one woman from the front row walking toward the back of the plane. She plopped down in the row ahead of me on the opposite side of the aircraft and proceeded to tell everyone one of the scariest things I'd ever heard while airborne: A man in the front of the plane was having a heart attack, and the flight attendants had told her to find an open seat.

My gut feeling instantly changed into outright nausea. At 35,000 feet in the air, a man was in need of immediate medical attention, and I was within thirty feet of him.

As I stated previously, my awareness of my surroundings is always heightened in tense situations, and I will further this comment to say that medical emergencies are beyond my threshold of tolerance. I've never been able to keep calm when someone is having an issue that I have no control over. As my brain registered what was going on in the first aisle of the plane, I felt my stomach immediately churn.

My mouth grew dry, and I had an overwhelming feeling of nausea. Because involuntary bodily functions are uncontrollable, for the most part, I did my best to redirect my mind. I stared down at my computer to compose myself. The last thing the crew needed was a panicking passenger vomiting all over the place, and I knew I needed to calm down.

As soon as I looked down at my monitor, the lead flight attendant picked up the microphone and shouted over the intercom that all flight attendants needed to report to the front of the airplane for a medical emergency. She also asked any doctors onboard to come forward to provide their services. Although pretty much every passenger already knew something was wrong, that announcement was the proverbial stake to the heart, and the feeling in my stomach worsened.

The next ten to fifteen minutes were a blur of terrifying

events. The crew worked to stabilize the gentleman, pulling a plethora of medical equipment down from the overhead bins. I saw stethoscopes, a first aid kit, and plenty of gauze flying around, though I made my best effort not to stare directly toward him out of respect for his privacy and the preservation of my own sanity.

Unfortunately, that was easier said than done. Even with no control in the situation, my natural curiosity demanded that I know what was going on. I kept my attention on the man for part of the time and noticed that he was still able to breathe. From my angle, it did not appear as though his situation was worsening, and that thought helped my stomach to calm a bit. I so badly wanted the pilot to land so the man could go to the hospital for proper medical care.

Two men were seated in my row, so I turned to them and began a conversation, longing for some sense of camaraderie in a tense situation.

The man seated right next to me was wearing a Western hat, black cowboy boots, and old, tattered jeans. His button-down shirt was adorned with a bolo tie. Since I was headed to Texas, I generalized that he was on his way back to the state, and speaking with him only confirmed that assumption. In a thick Southern accent, he leaned over to me and expressed his sympathy for the man suffering in the front row, and I agreed and told him I hoped he would be okay.

Time passed far too slowly, as if we were stuck in a lapse, and everything was moving incredibly, painfully slowly. I daydreamt about all of the negative possibilities that might occur. My mind raced, and I worried that the man in front might actually die. I imagined complete chaos on the airplane, everyone frantically trying to help or freaking out. It was not a good feeling at thousands of feet above land.

All of a sudden, the plane jerked my body backward against the seat. We accelerated rapidly, and that jolt shook me out of my inner thoughts and back to reality. I heard the engines on both sides of the airplane roar with powerful force, not their standard sound at all. Typically, there is a muffled buzzing sound, a heavy noise of air flowing rapidly past the wings similar to the suction noise of a vacuum.

As the pilot changed the speed of the aircraft, the engines charged with energy, and the shift was noticeably loud in the cabin. Passengers snickered about the jolt as we propelled forward. A moment later, the pilot announced that we were going to make an emergency landing in Springfield, Missouri, the nearest airport, and that we'd be on the ground within a few minutes. A second later, I could feel the plane drop as an indicator of the promised descent.

The flight attendants shuffled frantically around the cabin, all except for one, who remained by the ailing man's side for the remainder of the flight and landing. All passengers were instructed to stay seated until further notice, and everyone sat quietly, their eyes trained on the man at the front, who looked absolutely miserable.

It is awful to be sick or to suffer any medical issue in any situation, and I certainly did not envy that man and the helpless position he was in. His life was being threatened with a heart attack, and there was nothing anyone onboard could do about it. All he and his family could do was wait until they reached Earth again. The vulnerability of his critical situation was at the mercy of the flight crew.

The employees of A+ Airlines worked to secure everything in the cabin. The passengers sat silently and waited until we felt the wheels of the plane touch the ground. The descent was much quicker than normal, and we were on the ground within minutes of the announcement, as promised, met by fire trucks, ambulances, and medical officials at the gate. The doors flew open, and the man was surrounded. He was bombarded with questions, pokes, and prods as they prepared to take him to the hospital. He was carried off the airplane on a stretcher within seconds of pulling into the gate.

As the commotion settled down, the pilot exited the cabin and made another announcement over the intercom, thanking us all for being patient, cooperative, and understanding. He then gave us the bad news that since the Springfield airport was not one that A+ Airlines typically flew into, there would be a delay of at least two hours to complete all necessary paperwork, a requirement of the FAA and the parent company. Some passengers murmured sighs of annoyance, but I continued to listen.

We were told that we could use the restroom aboard the plane, but no one was allowed to get off the jet. The flight attendants would circle through the cabin and offer water to anyone who needed it while we waited.

Passengers scoffed at the inconvenience of, an entirely an unpredictable situation. The man next to me summed up the entire fiasco perfectly when he said he would hope that if it were one of his loved ones, they would do the exact same thing for him. I couldn't have agreed more. I would have taken an eight-hour delay* any day over a heart attack. As I sat there and waited to head back into the clouds, I began to reflect on what we'd just been through.

Thinking about what happened to "Jack" made me think of my own family. I couldn't fathom the fear that he and his loved ones had to go through, held hostage by helplessness in such a dire situation. If such a thing ever happens to one of my loved ones, I would hope for a similar response. Jack's life was in immediate danger. He'd walked onto that flight thinking he would land safely at his destination, but within a few moments, his life changed drastically.

I then remembered the weird gut feeling I'd felt that morning. Something within my body instinctually knew that something on the flight was going to be amiss. My mother's wisdom resurfaced once again, and the gut feeling I felt was spot-on. Deep within me, I knew something different was going to happen that day. I couldn't have ever predicted it would be

---

* Since I exaggerate, I should note that the actual delay was only two hours. The pilots made up for the lag in time a little during the second leg of the flight. I have had weather delays that have been far worse.

something like that, because I'm not a psychic), but I believe instinct played a major role in my feelings that day. Just like the time when I chose a guy over my girlfriend, my stomach ached to tell me something was off.

That experience taught me two very important lessons. First, it is important to take my mother's advice and listen to my gut. There really is no way of knowing when something negative will happen, but when my body sends me nonverbal signs, I listen to them. There's something to be said about that knot in my stomach that I feel every once and a while. It's my subconscious telling me I need to be on high alert.

For anyone who has ever experienced this phenomenon, you will know what I am talking about. It is difficult to describe the exact feeling. Only those who believe in it will have the opportunity to actually feel it. It is something I will continue to be cognizant of. My mother's advice at a young age was more valuable than I thought, and, as always, I sincerely appreciate her wisdom.

The second lesson I gleaned from that experience is that we can never take our health for granted. Jack was an elderly gentleman, but medical emergencies can occur for anyone, anytime, anywhere. They can sneak up on us, and all we can do when they happen is react. It is important to be as cautious and prepared as possible, because anything can happen. It could have been anyone on that airplane. It could have been me, and that is something I will forever consider in my future.

I am thankful that none of the people I care about most have been put in a similar situation. Anytime some sort of medical issue has come up, we have been in the vicinity of a hospital. I care deeply about my family and their wellbeing, and I know they feel the same about me. I hope all medical emergencies on planes can have as good of an ending as Jack's.

I am also grateful that the few medical emergencies I've endured have been negligible at worst. For the most part, I wake up each day feeling physically great. After an experience like this, I realized I take this for granted. I am tired many days, but I've reconsidered my complaints about that for my future.* The ability to wake up with energy, spunk, and a zest for life are priceless – a luxury that is not enjoyed by everyone. I try to remind myself of this often.

I'm not sure if Jack survived the incident, and I only know he was alive when he was carefully escorted off the plane. That is how I relive the experience in my head, and I wish him and his family the best.

After that traumatic experience, I truly learned to trust my gut. I know what I felt that day, and the feeling became even more real when I saw him suffering. I always have a good reminder of my mother's lesson each and every time my stomach drops. Although it took me a little longer to fully understand the meaning, it is now as clear as a bright, blue-sky day. There is no mistaking instinct; it's trusting instinct that is the hard part.

---

*   This does not mean I won't complain about being tired in the future, as it is almost a daily occurrence. I will, however, think about how good I feel compared to what my health could be. Being tired is something I subject myself to by finding other activities to pass my time instead of getting a proper night's rest.

Chapter Seventeen

The Final Descent

For as much as I've learned throughout my hundreds, or maybe thousands, of flights, I still manage to meet someone brand new every time. There is always a new story, problem, dream, or wish that crosses my path. I appreciate the diversity among my fellow passengers. Everyone has a story to tell, be it negative or positive. Each and every story in this book has been included because they have left a lasting impression, engraved an emotional stamp in my memory, some good and some bad.

The final story, Jack's story, was rather frightening. Being confined to a metal object moving at 450 miles per hour while someone was exceptionally ill scared me half to death. I didn't want to end the book on such a negative note, so I thought about rearranging the chapters to begin and end with uplifting tales and feel-good, happy-ending stories. In the end, I chose not to do this, for manufactured happily-ever-afters have a tendency to taint reality.

I compiled each and every one of these for a reason: Each has some sort of memory, thought, or feeling attached to it. I wrote them as they inspired me individually rather than forcing them into some sort of unnatural order just to make a better book.

When I initially told these stories to my friends, family, colleagues (and really anyone else who would listen) one at a time, I got an overwhelming and unexpected response. People had a "something similar happened to me" reaction, and they would proceed to tell me their own stories. I have to admit, none of them really revolved around airplanes, but the cohesion of like stories about influential strangers was genuine. It made me rethink the entire slew of the people that I had met over the years.

Everyone can assimilate with the paternal protection offered up by Howard. His generosity, fatherly instincts, and sincerity were honorable. It made me think of my own father, and the handful of men in my life who I have looked up to as role models. These people are invaluable. I only hope that Howard and each of the thousands of people he crossed in his travels realized just what a gem he was.

Any American citizen would be privileged to sit beside John and hear him swoon over his gorgeous family. Someone who devoted their life for the good of others is more than just a soldier. He set a selfless example of courage, commitment, and martyrdom to be appreciated and thought about by me for the rest of my life. His children, wife, and parents should be thanked over and over again as well. I'm sure they couldn't be more proud.

Kenny was that guy you meet once in a lifetime. He was the kind of person that cared enough to save a pearl earring while jumping out of a plane, and he managed to get it all on video to make a great story at the end of it. Mandy is the person who motivated others to better their life and in the process bettered hers. Her self-confidence and poise is something to adore.

Harry was an important reminder that no matter how successful a person is it is critical to remember their roots. The value of a good reputation far outweighs any championship game or best in class record. Both things will go down in history, but a person's reputation can be tarnished at the lost sight of their beginnings.

People have even encountered the "Marks" in the world. These are the people whose unhappiness seeps from their pores. They try to push their problems off on others and blame the people they care the most about for being the root of their problem. In cases like him, it is helpful to reflect on the positives in life. Mark's impact on me was just as important as any of the uplifting stories. The good in life makes the bad worth the temporary ailments.

I only hope that everyone has experiences like I did while floating through the atmosphere. Whether it is in a park, on public transportation, at the grocery store, in a social interest group, or even alongside volunteers to help rebuild the victim's homes of Hurricane Katrina, there is no right or wrong place (or a bad time) for others to create memories. Each builds upon the ones before it, capturing the moment at that given time. For me, these flights were well worth the hours of sitting in a hard leather chair bound by the limit of space. I was meant to meet these people.

It seems as though there really isn't a well-known proper etiquette for behavior on airplanes. For some strange reason, people tend to forget how to behave the minute they step onboard. I am never ceased to be amazed with some of the things I see and hear. As you may have noticed throughout these stories, I have come across the good, the bad, and the ugly. There are so many stories that are not included here, but they all have something to say.

I recognize that I am not the only person who has documented airplane craziness. There are hundreds of blogs, websites, and Internet forums directly linked to unusual aircraft experiences. One story described how a man put his annoying child in the overhead compartment halfway through a flight to reduce the noise. Another mentioned a passenger who refused to put clothing on once he was airborne. On a monthly average, there is at least one form of craziness that pops up on the local television news channel.

Southwest Airlines, a company I have the utmost respect for and commend for their outstanding business model, has partnered with The Learning Channel (TLC) for *On the Fly,* the airline's depiction of the daily trials and tribulations of the traveling world. Southwest Airlines employees and passengers are followed with a camera crew to some of their busiest hubs across the country. The daily struggles, problems, highlights, and lowlights are all broadcasted for the world to view right from the comfort of their own home.

I've watched a few episodes, and I've come to one conclusion: Patience could, quite possibly, be an airline personnel's greatest asset. Bearing this in mind, I'd like to thank the countless airline industry employees, from the flight attendants to the pilots to the hundreds of people behind the scenes who make a destination thousands of miles away flawlessly accessible. Without these hardworking, patient people, traveling to new destinations would not be a simple process.

Passengers often forget about all the people who work to get them safely to their destinations. I've sat in airports for eight hours at a time, waiting for a delayed flight to take me home after a grueling work week. I've missed plenty of flights and been told I would not get on another one until hours later. I've witnessed grown adults throwing temper tantrums because they were told something they did not want to hear. I'm only a passenger on these flights, so I can only imagine what the people who work for their airlines experience every day.

It is important to remember that no matter how well one plans, life can and does get in the way. There will always be horrific weather patterns, disruptive patrons, short-staffed crews, and mechanical issues to contend with. Things happen, and it is better to roll with the punches than to fight them. This lesson is learned quickly when a person flies frequently.

At the beginning of this book, I described a small portion of my childhood. I told you about the bully who worked so hard to make my days at school a little more challenging. I was and still very much am a teacher's pet. I still aim to please authority in any degree I can. The difference is my perspective on my position. Neither stereotype is right or wrong. I am still learning who I am each day of my life, but the teacher's pet identity has just sort of stuck with me consistently.

In the grand scheme of things, it doesn't matter if you are the teacher's pet or the class bully. Though it seemed like it was all that mattered in elementary school, people are people, regardless of the labels we put on ourselves or others put on us. We all have a place in society, despite the stereotypes we are categorized into. The challenge is to learn how to accept attributes and flaws as equally important, for all of these are what shape an individual, and we all have them.

To this point, one of the most impactful lessons I have learned throughout the process of flying is that the connection with humanity is binding, despite one's origination or destination. For a long while, I mistakenly assumed that every person on the airplane with me in Chicago had originated there. It made sense to me that if we all got on at the same location, everyone *must have* started their journey there. I've learned that this is just not true.

With all of the connecting flights, layovers, airplane changes, switches, delays, cancelations, and other complicated logistics that drive the airline industry, there really is no telling who you will sit next to. A fellow passenger could live 10 miles from you or 10,000 miles from you. One just never knows.

The world really is a small place. I've met people from all over, some from far away, and some who were from places closer to me than I ever imagined, like the man who lived a few miles from my house and ran on the same trail I did, with a daughter who attended the same college as me. Another man indulged in the same local Italian joints in my neighborhood. We sat around talking about the best appetizers that we both enjoyed for an hour during one random flight.

One woman I sat next to randomly knew my father and had grown up just two blocks away from him on the south side of Chicago. She sat one row behind him during grammar school and remembered what a trouble-maker he was. It's funny how some things never change. Somehow we, as people, are all connected.

That is the essence of travel. Someone can be flying from the most remote location in the world, and you could end up sitting next to them. There is a sense of camaraderie as you join the people heading to the same destination as you on an airplane. You never know what you might learn, even if the lesson is on a paper airplane that hits you in the head.

I'll never forget that day in fifth grade. Getting hit in the head by that A+ Airlines paper airplane was one of the best things that could have happened to me. Obviously, it made a greater impact on me than that bully ever intended. I learned *the value of a message.*

I also learned that a message can be delivered in the strangest of ways by people who are totally unexpected. The examples in this book are tangible proof of that. I boarded the flights mentioned in this book with my only expectations being transportation from Point A to Point B. In retrospect, I received quite a bit more than I bargained for.

Each of these stories has impacted my life in some way or another. I believe the individuals I've interacted with were put in my life to teach me many important lessons. I walked away from each and every one of those people with a new perspective.

I'm not convinced that the mayhem I've endured on my many flights was rare in the airline industry. I've seen much worse in *On the Fly* episodes and read about them in some of the blogs on Internet. The abnormalities in this book are just the daily foes that occur in the airline industry. Almost everyone has a story that starts with the phrase, "I remember this one crazy flight when…" followed by some off-the-wall anecdote. In other words, hundreds of stories precede those included in this book.

I didn't experience the first crazy thing on an airplane, and I won't be the last. One thing I do know is that my individual experiences were indeed special. Each of the individuals who made them that way influenced my life more than they will ever know. Each one created a lasting memory that I was able to re-create and share here, with you, and I am grateful for all of them. This is my collection of unique tales from a mile high.

Ladies and gentlemen, in preparation for our final decent and landing, the captain has turned the "Fasten Seatbelt" sign back on. Please lock your tray tables in the upright position and gather your garbage together. The flight attendants will be coming through the cabin to make one last pass to collect anything you do not want to take with you off the plane. We want to thank you once again for choosing A+ Airlines. We will be on the ground shortly. We hope you've enjoyed your flight. Welcome to your destination...

Epilogue

My experiences on airplanes are at the forefront of my tenure. I am a veteran flyer at a young age, and I will continue to spend time on jets. The notion that my stories have only just begun excites me to no end whether I experience them on an airplane or not. I'm sure that my collection of stories will continue to grow exponentially with the years to come under my belt. The stories in this book are a mere foundation for the rest of my life.

The purpose of any book is to be successful, but every author defines that in their own way. For me, there are a few goals that I have for this book. I have outlined them below. I will preface these goals by saying that even if none of them are fulfilled, the opportunity to write and publish this novel was success in itself for me.

My defined goals for this book bring a few distinct things to mind. The first is for readers to emotionally bond with the stories herein. The stories I chose for this book have touched me in a way that I will never forget. Each and every person mentioned deserves to be included. Their happiness, struggles, and lives are something I shared a part of. I could never compile a holistic list of the world's craziest things that occur on airplanes.[*] I respect the individuals I have flown with in the past, and I will continue to do so in the future. The characters are people I believed most readers could relate with and form a bond. I will know that I have accomplished something if even one reader laughs, cries, or remembers the stories I've shared in this book.

I've revealed tiny snippets of information about my family throughout parts of the book. As I've alluded to, my family loves to gather around a table and mull over old and new stories. I have spent hours as a child and an adult telling and listening to such anecdotes. Everyone refills their drink and laughs until our stomachs hurt for hours. These times are some of the most cherished in my life. The time I spend with my family is invaluable. I look forward to each and every party, with the same people over and over again.

Any passenger who has ever experience a special story while flying, which probably includes the majority of the airborne population, will remember their own unique situation. I hope my experiences spark memories of these tales. I hope these anecdotes bring as much joy and laughter to your family as they have mine. The thought of hundreds or even thousands of readers enjoying time with their family is an opportunistic one.

My third goal for this book is to inspire other authors to publish their stories. I'm not suggesting that every author should compose a book about flying, airplanes, or anything else that is included in this book. Instead, I challenge the writers to share their own unique stories. Ask yourself what drives you to get up in the morning and start writing it down. At their core, people are all unique individuals. Everyone has their own likes, dislikes, favorites, passions, hobbies, beliefs, rules, etcetera. Let those

---

[*]   There are a few websites and blogs designated just to report the wild things that happen on airplanes. I found the most thorough reports at www.flightsfromhell.com and an annual report of the top ten flight disasters on www.onlinetravelreview.com. These two sites do a phenomenal job of keeping up to date and reporting some of the most interesting snippets.

things be your vice. Take what you know and put it on paper. You'll be surprised how far you can get writing about something you love. Who knows? You might even have fun with it!

My final goal for this book is to one day encounter someone reading it on an airplane, even if it is twenty years from now. When I envision the epitome of success, this is exactly what comes to mind. The accomplishment of knowing that people are enjoying the written work that I put so much effort into is a reward in and of itself. Part of the irony of this book is that all of the stories took place on, around, near, or in association with an airplane. I want to walk onto a jet with no expectations, sit down, and be asked by the person next to me, "Have you read this? It's called *paper airplane.*"

Acknowledgments

This book was a compilation of events and experiences courtesy of people who may never know they've been highlighted in these pages. Everyone herein played an essential part in my writing process, whether they know it or not – not only because they helped to create a story, but because they made a lasting impression on me that I felt compelled to share. I am forever grateful to these, and I sincerely look forward to the hundreds of others I will meet in my lifetime and my travels. I'm sure each one will contribute to my plethora of knowledge.

I would also like to personally thank my friends for supporting me in each and every one of my endeavors. They help me through each feat and are always willing to help me relieve stress at the local watering hole. I am lucky enough to be surrounded by friends whom I consider to be my family. They always know how to make any situation better, and I can always count on them to defend the silver lining.

My parents have encouraged me unconditionally throughout my life, and I am proud to write this book in their honor. My entire life has been a treat, and I have them to thank for that. Thank you so very much, Mom and Dad, for always being my biggest fans.

I want to thank my sister Stephanie, aka "Cookies." Without such a role model, I would not be the person I am today, nor would I ever initiate volunteering. She sets an example for others without even trying. Her good nature, genius mind, and insatiable laugh will take her far, and I'm glad to go along for the ride. I couldn't ask for a better best friend and supporter. Love you, Cooks.

I want to thank the love of my life, Joseph. I've never met someone who has cared more about my happiness than you do. You are my best friend, my perfect counterpart. Thank you for being in my life. I feel more than blessed to have met such an important person at such a young age. Many people never meet their soul mate. I think it's more than luck that I have met mine, and I'm so excited to live my life with you.

About The Author

Kersten L. Kelly is a self-published author of narrative nonfiction and semi-fiction books. She grew up in Munster, Indiana and currently works in a sales role based out of Chicago, Illinois. She started writing at an early age and graduated from Indiana University with a dual bachelor's degree in economics and communication and culture. She then went on to earn a master's in business administration from the Kelley School of Business at Indiana University.

She has a passion for learning, teaching, and writing. In her spare time, she enjoys international travel with her friends and family and training for running events of various distances. She likes the outdoors, social media, pop culture, and any new technologies that draw the people of the world a little bit closer together. She can be reached via e-mail at KerstenLKelly@gmail.com or through the Talisman Book Publishing website at www.TalismanBookPublishing.com.

Want more? Scan our QR code.

www.talismanbookpublishing.com

Talisman Book Publishing LLC is an organic company devoted to publishing, promoting, and reviewing books of all genres in both paperback and eBook format. Kersten L. Kelly founded the company when she wrote and published her first book *ec·o·nom·ics: a simple twist on normalcy* in March 2012. She wanted to retain the rights and be an intrinsic influence on each step of the process of publishing the book. She chose to pave her own path and did not query any major publishing companies. Instead, she started at ground zero and created a publishing company to back her hard work and dedication to her writing. She hasn't looked back since.

Kersten learned quite a bit through the process and wanted to help others who are beginning authors in the industry. TBP specializes in helping authors who are interested in self-publishing get a strong foundation for their process. Marketing a book takes ample time and effort, and we are here to help create a venue to do that. Our goal is to work together with bloggers, authors, readers, reviewers, and any other book enthusiasts to publish and promote books successfully.

www.ingramcontent.com/pod-product-compliance
Lightning Source LLC
Chambersburg PA
CBHW070821180626
46818CB00001B/353